AGAINST AN ALPINE SKY

NICOLE LELAND

Book Cover by Asterielly Designs
(https://www.asteriellydesigns.com)

Chapter Header Art by ElenaDoroshArt

Scene Break Art by sketchify

Content Note

Against an Alpine Sky is a fantasy romance between a human woman and a stone man set in the mountains of a secondary fantasy world. While the romance is overall gentle and sweet, this story does include elements that may be upsetting to some readers. These include:

- Depiction of an abusive relationship (physical, emotional)
- Sexual harassment
- Infertility
- Sexism
- Racism against other sentient species

Readers who are sensitive to these topics, please be aware and take care of yourselves.

Dedication

For my mom, who was always so supportive of my writing and believed I would someday be a "famous" author.

She would have loved this book.

♥

Chapter One

Catching a bee without harming it was no easy task, especially when your hands were made of stone. But Talos was patient and determined. No bees would die between his fingers—not this time.

He tracked the honeybee as it landed on a nearby lupine. Carefully, he positioned his small net to catch the bee as it reemerged from the flower. It buzzed, confused and unhappy, as it found itself trapped. Gentle as the wind, Talos used his granite fingers to pinch the end of the net closed and trap the bee inside. He watched the honeybee buzz its wings in irritation as it crawled around and around the enclosed space.

"Hello, my pretty." He smiled, captivated by the waving antennae, the bristly hairs, the swollen yellow pollen baskets, the beautifully veined wings. Insects were endlessly fascinating and varied. He yearned to put the bee in a glass jar and get his sketchbook, to immortalize every hair and segment in charcoal or graphite, but he had other plans for this bee.

Carefully using string to tie the net closed, he secured it alongside the dozen others already on his back and started climbing back up the rocks toward home. He passed Raffa's cart on the track just beyond their stone patio, then the doorway to their living space set into the side of the mountain, and heard the faint sounds of Raffa swearing to himself and crashing around inside. He moved up beyond the patio and climbed further, to the rugged stone ledges above where he had carried soil and wild strawberry plants to build his own little garden on the rocks.

The low tangles of strawberry runners and lush three-part leaves were dotted with white and yellow flowers and the occasional ruby red gem of a ripening fruit. It was hot and dry here on the rocks, and he would need to water the plants again today. The woven grass canopy that gave them some relief from the blistering sun needed another patch soon, too. But having the plants close enough for careful daily observation made the extra maintenance work worth it.

The fruits were small and sometimes misshapen. Talos had a theory it was because the flowers weren't adequately pollinated. With the gentle attention of these bees, he suspected that would change.

"I hope you like strawberry flower nectar." He released one bee into each of the cages he had set around some of his plants. The bees buzzed around the enclosures, getting used to the new space and spreading their wings after their confinement. Talos smiled to see some of them start to land on the white flowers, sticking their heads deep to lap up the nectar there—and getting covered in downy yellow pollen.

Talos had finished recording the notes for his experiment and was in the middle of sketching a honeybee as it visited a strawberry flower, spending extra care on the details of how the bee's tongue fit down into the glistening nectaries, when Raffa yelled his name. Talos flinched, then sighed, setting his journal aside.

"I'm up here," he called back, walking to sit on the edge of his rock ledge and look at his brother below.

The other lithander was both taller and broader than Talos, rough gray except for his black flint eyes. Their father had carved Raffa during the last war, and the vestiges of the time period were self-evident. Raffa looked like a cross between a stone bear and a giant wolf, with the benefit of opposable thumbs and knuckles lined with long claws. Talos, who had been crafted decades later, was much sleeker and more fanciful—a human form with the wings of a bird and long waves of feathers draping down his back like hair. The lighter toned granite he'd been carved from looked almost white compared to Raffa.

Raffa looked up with a scowl that showed all his carved, predatory teeth. "Are you wasting time on those flowers again?"

"I like them."

"Waste of time," Raffa said again. "It's not like we eat them."

"That's not the point," Talos said, but he'd had this same argument with his brother too many times already. Raffa was as blunt and stolid as the granite he was carved from, and Talos had so far failed to impress upon him the beauty and curiosity and magic of living things. He sighed, his stone wings fluttering restlessly. "Are you leaving? I'll come down."

Raffa grunted, and Talos took that as a yes, climbing from his perch to the flat patio below. A bag had been added to the otherwise empty cart, one bursting with stone working tools.

"Did you decide between Rocheburg or the quarries in South Shaleside?" Talos asked.

"South Shaleside," Raffa said, testing the sharpness of his knuckle claws against the wood of the cart. "Rocheburg's granite is running out, and they've been trying to pass off inferior feldspar garbage for the same prices. Damn Desroches."

"You'll be gone two weeks?"

"Sounds about right."

Talos nodded, feeling awkward. His brother was beginning a vital part of the lithander life: picking out the stone to carve his own child. Talos was trying to be supportive. He had helped Raffa with sketches of potential forms for when he began carving and even let him flip through his sketchbooks of various animals for inspiration. But the idea of creating a new life, of laboring over stone choice and design and carving, of imbuing the form with a piece of his own lifeforce to give it a semblance of life—the idea of creating a new sentient being—intimidated Talos. People were complicated, whether they were made of flesh or stone. Creating a new person felt like a dangerous gamble, and Raffa's driving desire to do so felt foreign to Talos. Maybe it was the difference between having fought in a war against humans and not.

"Good luck," he said. It came out half question.

Raffa scowled. "You should be building up your animas magic and thinking about your own son, not wandering the countryside and drawing pictures of flowers."

Yes, this was definitely a sore spot between them. But then, despite being brothers, Talos and Raffa had very little in common.

"Safe travels, brother."

"Don't worry. I can make my travels safe," Raffa said, folding his fingers into fists so his claws stood straight and sharp.

When Raffa was finally out of sight, pulling his cart behind him, Talos climbed back to his strawberries. The bees had lost interest in the flowers, crawling on the undersides of the cages instead, sated and longing for home. Talos felt the opposite. A restlessness was in him, and he had no desire to go inside and deal with the mess Raffa had no doubt left in the wake of his packing. Ruffling his stone wings, he tipped the cages over one after another, letting the bees free. Then he packed a satchel for a hike.

Chapter Two

I t was as Maëlle came out of the library, cheerful for the first time in days, that Gaubert cornered her.

Her arms were full of blocky, leather-bound books, each spine embossed with a small version of the Desroches family crest. They must be custom copies—such a luxury! The creamy pages barely looked touched, and Maëlle couldn't help but wonder if they were used more as a status symbol than for reading. All the better for her, she decided, wide skirts swishing through the library's door and into the manor's wide hallway while singing quietly to herself. She could at least be happy with all the new books she could read, even if she was unhappy with everything else these days.

She almost walked right into Gaubert outside the library, and her singing immediately cut off in a gasp of surprise. He gave her a grin that she was sure many women found charming. She mostly found it smarmy.

"I thought I would find you here," he said. "Followed the sound of your squawking." It wasn't even noon yet, and already his breath was touched with the scent of honeyed wine. He braced a hand against the brocade tapestry on the wall next to her, trapping her in place.

"You don't like my singing," she said.

He shrugged. "Women should be seen, not heard." He leaned closer, his hot breath damp on her neck. "But if you insist on making noise, I could give you something much better to squawk about." His free hand rested possessively on her hip, trying to draw her against him.

"Gaubert!" Maëlle said, trying to move her stack of books more solidly between herself and her fiancé. She wanted her tone to sound scandalized, but was sure it came across more as panicked. "We're not married yet. It's improper for you to touch me so familiarly."

She looked around, past Gaubert's close bulk, trying to find the silhouette of Gaubert's Aunt Pruen, who was ostensibly acting as Maëlle's chaperone. Maëlle didn't have any living female relatives of her own, but her father had been happy to accept Aunt Pruen as chaperone during her court-ingmoon with Gaubert. It had seemed like a good idea at the time—both the courtingmoon to become accustomed to her arranged fiancé and his manor before their official marriage and having his aunt as chaperone. But the woman, it turned out, was over ninety, half blind, and slept more than an old cat. She made a terrible chaperone.

Gaubert seemed to prefer it that way.

"Only two more weeks," he said. He leaned closer, smelling the sweet violet oil in her hair. The crimson silk of his sleeve brushed against her ear, and she shivered. "Even if my seed took, no one would think a baby born two weeks early was anything unusual."

Maëlle felt her whole body go cold and clammy. He was being beyond improper now. She had never had a particu-larly strong interest in sex, but Gaubert's behavior over the last two weeks was making her actively dread the idea.

"You're pretty enough," he continued, giving that same cocky grin again. "I would make sure the experience wasn't all chore for you."

She felt like she was suffocating. Trapped. Not just by the mass of muscle and smirk currently pinning her to a wall, but by everything—her arranged marriage, her responsibilities as wife, the expectation of children, her duties as daughter, the stony prison of this ancient manor house. She needed air. She needed out.

"I have to go," she tried, looking for some gap between Gaubert and the empty hallway beyond.

"Shy little thing, aren't you?"

"You're making me uncomfortable, Gaubert."

He shrugged those broad shoulders of his. "Soon enough, it will be your duty, uncomfortable or not."

"But not yet today."

His smirk turned more scowl, and she couldn't take it any longer. She twisted, 'accidentally' jamming the sharp corner of the biggest book she carried into his ribs. He winced, pulling back, and she took the moment to slip under his arm and into the clear. She was halfway down the hall already before he straightened and called after her.

"Soon enough, Maëlle."

She rounded the corner and almost collapsed against the nearby wall, trying to suppress the shivers. This part of the hallway was lined with tall windows, currently propped open for the sake of fresh air. The sunlight slanted through glass and gaps alike, leaving stripes on the stone floor like bars of a prison. Maëlle gave herself a count of fifty to cringe and feel weak, to feel sorry for herself. Then she made herself stand straight and tall. She could do this. She had to.

Just...not today.

The song of birds filtered in through the windows, flitting easy and free among the honeysuckle vines. The smell of the flowers was cloyingly sweet—too many planted too close, trained to grow up wrought iron trellises on the manor's outer walls. In the distance, the Rochesne Mountains painted the horizon, purpled in the late morning light.

Changing directions, she headed down the covered walkway towards the stables instead of to her rooms, calling for one of the stable hands to saddle Arwa for her. She sent one of the servants for a loaf of bread, a couple of apples, and a bottle of wine from the kitchen. She needed air and space and distance from her fiancé. She would ride somewhere quiet and spend the day reading in the peace of nature, away from Gaubert's eyes and hands and intentions.

"Hey, lovely," Maëlle said, running familiar hands down Arwa's neck feathers in just the way she liked. Arwa cooed happily, leaning down to rustle affectionately in Maëlle's hair with her beak.

Arwa was an owl gryphon, with the heart shaped face of a barn owl and the black and white spots of a bobcat. Maëlle had had her since she was ten; it was common for nobles to learn to ride gryphons instead of or in addition to horses in the northern forests, and Arwa had been her first. Assuming nothing injured her, Arwa might live to be as old as Maëlle herself. Maëlle hoped she would; the gryphon was the closest thing she had to a friend.

Ten minutes later, a bag slung over her back, Maëlle was in the air. She always loved this part. The wind in her hair and the ground spread out like a living map beneath her feet, she pressed into Arwa's warm feathers while the snap of wings held them aloft. It felt like freedom and living and sweetness all rolled into one.

She guided Arwa towards the mountains to the east. The craggy peaks were oddly comforting, more like her home to the north than anywhere else near Gaubert's manor. The higher elevations even had the same kind of spruces and pines as the grounds at home.

Maëlle found one such pine, standing tall atop a moss and lichen topped rock, and made herself comfortable. She had a wool blanket to wrap up in, her lunch provisions, and several good books to read. The only real question was whether she would be more distracted by a novel or a political history today. Running a hand over the cover of the history book she had brought, she noticed Gaubert's family crest among those painted on the leather cover. She swallowed hard, tucking the book away. Novel it was, apparently.

It was a beautiful sunny day, and though there was a chill breeze at this elevation, she didn't mind. The possibility that she could escape to these mountains even after her marriage to Gaubert was the only thing that kept her sane on some days. She wouldn't let him take away Arwa, or this tiny piece of freedom.

Her marriage to Gaubert Desroches had been arranged by her father fully two years ago, not long after her mother had died. The Desroches family was one with a well-respected name and the kind of political clout Maëlle's father had always aspired to. The Desroches coffers, on the other hand, had grown thin in recent years. Their granite pits had been mostly exhausted, and the few gem mines that had been running in the mountains for decades brought out fewer gems every year. That combined with the apparent inability of the Desroches heirs to practice anything approaching frugality had left them hungry for a marriage that would bring them money. Maëlle offered that—or rather, her father and his burgeoning wealth as a gryphon breeder offered that.

She sometimes thought her father saw her as nothing more than another piece of livestock to be bartered away. Or maybe that was unfair; she could, theoretically, have a comfortable and rich life here with Gaubert. If only he wasn't such an uncouth cad.

She sighed, realizing she hadn't retained a single word of the first five pages she had read in the novel. Maybe reading wouldn't be enough to distract her today after all.

Maëlle turned fond eyes on Arwa, letting herself be distracted by the owl gryphon stalking through a stand of alder. Arwa had been prowling around the area, creeping in bushes and chasing up songbirds and mice for the sport. She was the size of a horse, despite her more modest cat ancestor, and it still surprised Maëlle sometimes how quiet the gryphon could be.

Arwa tensed suddenly, owl head turning smoothly to look toward one edge of the rock ledge they sat on. Her dark eyes sharpened, like she had seen larger prey. Maëlle wondered what it might be. A racoon, maybe? Or goat or cougar? Maëlle felt no fear. Even a bear would be no match for Arwa, and the gryphon had a protective streak that ran deeper than bone.

She turned to her book again, flipping back to the first page in hopes of catching the words this time around, letting Arwa hunt as she pleased. But when she heard a man's voice of alarm from the direction Arwa had gone, she leapt to her feet.

Chapter Three

Talos ran his granite tongue over the rock, wishing not for the first time that he had tastebuds. Some minerals were easiest to identify by taste; he had read as much in one of the many human books he had at home. He stared at the pink crystals in the rock he held, wondering if they were halite or sylvite. Either way, they made a fascinating crystalline pattern. Maybe he would sketch the rock.

A noise caught his attention—some animal moving around and rustling through bushes on a rocky ledge just to the other side of the nearby chasm. It was a large enough ledge that it held several trees, and the edge closest to him was lined with shrubs, obstructing his view of what made the noise. It sounded halfway between the snuffle of a cat and the coo of a bird. The way the brush moved in its wake made it seem large.

Talos walked closer, peering in the direction of the noise as if he could see through the shrubs. A moment later, a twitch of movement caught his attention. A rustle of gray-spotted white wings, larger than any bird he had ever seen, lifted briefly above the leaves. What had wings that broad? Bigger than an owl or an eagle. A harpy, maybe? They sometimes migrated through the mountains here. There was another rustle of movement, and this time, a spotted furry rump with a short snub tail made an appearance. It looked like a very large bobcat—but with wings?

Was it a gryphon?

He looked once more at his rock before dropping it back to the ground. He had never seen a gryphon before. They were rare and majestic beasts, more common in the forests to the north. If there was a gryphon here... He yearned to get a closer look, to take notes and make sketches and see the animal for himself. Adjusting his bag across his chest, he started carefully climbing through the deep rocky crevice to get closer to the rock ledge.

Almost to the top, Talos stopped on a smaller ledge, hoping for a glimpse of the animal before he spooked it. He was just grasping branches of alder and blueberry to move them aside when a face the size of a bear's pushed abruptly through the foliage, and a hooked beak launched at his nose.

He let out a cry of alarm, surprised by the closeness and the suddenness and the angry violence with which the gryphon tried to dislodge him. If he hadn't already been holding onto the branches of shrubs, he may have lost his balance and fallen into the chasm below.

The heart-shaped face pulled back and cocked to the side, considering him. Then the gryphon hissed and lunged again. Talos ducked, scrabbling to keep his footing. What would he do if the gryphon actually caught him?

"Arwa! Heel!" The voice rang out, clear and bright, the sound striking a cord in Talos he didn't expect. A human voice. He froze.

The gryphon hissed again, but to Talos's relief, the beast pulled its head back through the shrubs and disappeared. A second later, a human face appeared in its place. Presumably, the owner of the voice.

Talos had always admired the amount of color in humans. Lithander were limited to a stone palette, mostly grays and blacks and whites for the sake of their commonness. But even discounting their colorful clothes, humans were painted with colors of their own. This human—a woman, he felt fairly sure—had hair the golden color of honey with amber highlights, skin the pale brown of ash wood, and eyes as deep and blue as glacial lakes.

"Oh!" she said, spying him on the ledge. "A lithander?"

For a moment, Talos considered running. He had no doubt he could climb these mountain cliffs faster than this more fragile human, and it seemed unlikely that she would make the effort to follow on her gryphon. Humans and lithander had never been excellent friends and had fought on opposite sides during the last three wars. There may be a tenuous peace now, but most humans found the lithander alien and scary. Raffa's war stories only emphasized the differences between the two species. But to his surprise, instead of pulling back in fear or disgust, as he expected, the human woman extended him a hand.

"Are you ok? Arwa didn't hurt you, did she?"

He stared at her hand. Was she really offering him help? Considering he was carved of solid granite, there was no way she could hope to heft him to the ridge above. "Arwa is...the gryphon?" he asked.

"She was just protecting me," the woman said, giving a fond smile to the gryphon. She reached back, ruffling Arwa's neck feathers until the gryphon cooed in pleasure. "I promise she won't hurt you."

"I don't think she could."

"You'd be surprised. Arwa is quite clever."

Talos thought again about how he had almost lost his footing, almost fallen into the chasm below. He would have likely survived such a fall but may have been disfigured for the rest of his existence. Rock could break, after all. Talos had seen what happened to a lithander that split the granite of their body, the loss of a limb, the leaked animas magic. For a moment, he felt a strong pang of loss on behalf of his middle sibling, Sándor.

"Please come up," the woman said, offering her hand again with a soft smile. "I'll introduce you to Arwa properly."

Above, the gryphon let out a huff of air. A real gryphon—an owl gryphon, by the shape of her face. Talos may never have the chance to meet one again.

"Thank you," he said carefully, nodding to her hand. "But I will make my own way up."

The gryphon was even larger than he had expected, fully the size of a horse with a wingspan of more than twenty-five feet. She was beautiful, with an undercoat of white fur and feathers and a scattering of black spots and brown markings. Her wings and heart-shaped face were lined with warm brown tones, and her eyes were all black. The saddle strapped to her back was simple and clearly made for a custom fit.

The gryphon opened her beak and hissed, wings pulling open to their full span.

"Arwa, be nice!" the woman said, but there was humor in her tone.

"She's enchanting," Talos said. "I've never met a gryphon before."

"I've never met a lithander before," the woman replied. She was watching him almost as closely as he was watching the gryphon, and he felt suddenly self-conscious.

"We're rarer even than gryphons." It was why Raffa was so insistent on carving a son sooner rather than later—he hated that the humans outnumbered them so handily.

"How does stone have the flexibility for movement and speech?" She was looking at him so earnestly, her expression so open and curious, he felt a moment of kinship with this human.

"The same way a gryphon can carry so much weight, I presume. Magic."

"Animas magic?"

He raised an eyebrow in her direction. "You're well informed."

"I read about the lithander in a book. Oh—I have it with me!"

Talos smiled, infected by her pure enthusiasm. She went to the tall pine at one end of the rock ledge, rummaging in the wool blanket piled there until she found a bag. From inside, she pulled free a little leatherbound book, showing him the cover: "Magical Fauna of the Rochesne Mountains." Her cheeks suddenly colored pink, the hue of spring beauty blooms, and he guessed from the way she clutched the book to her chest that it meant she was embarrassed.

"I'm new to the area and trying to learn more. Since I will be living here." A darker expression crossed her face, a storm cloud blotting out the sun, and Talos felt the strange urge to shield her from it. Why did it bother him to see her unhappy? He had no idea how humans measured beauty, but he supposed she was pretty in the way of a spring flower. Tall and willowy, features so supple and small, brushed with soft colors and painted in sunlight. She looked so delicate and fragile. Maybe that was why he felt the urge to protect her.

"I've read that book before," Talos said quietly, feeling oddly shy. "It's incomplete." He fought with himself for a moment, but she seemed a kindred spirit of sorts, someone who appreciated knowledge and information and books. Before he could rethink his decision, he pulled one of his journals free and offered it to her. "I've been cataloging everything that lives in the Rochesne Mountains," he explained, voice soft.

She took the journal delicately, like she was afraid she might break it. When she opened it, her eyes went wide, a gasp parting her lips. He hadn't known human eyes could sparkle that way, but their blue shimmered like sunlight on water. He yearned to find a pigment blue enough just so he could paint her expression.

"Did you make these sketches yourself?" she asked, turning the journal to show him his drawings of indigo buntings, notes about their anatomy and biology penned neatly to one side. He nodded, and her eyes sparkled again. "They're beautiful! You're an artist."

"Thank you." He found himself looking down and away from her, unable to weather her compliments. His gaze landed on Arwa again as the gryphon preened one wing. "I would enjoy drawing Arwa. For my books."

"Really? I'd love it if you did." Arwa twitched her head to one side at a rustling sound, bounding into the shrubs after some small animal, and the woman laughed. "Assuming I can get her to sit still long enough."

There was a rumble in the distance, and they both turned to the west to see distant dark storm clouds on the horizon. Talos frowned. Lightning was one of the few things that could seriously hurt a lithander if it struck directly. Something about it interrupted the animas magic that gave them life.

"Another day, it seems," he said.

"Yes, I suppose we should both head home before the weather arrives." Why did she sound so sad saying that? Was that fear lacing her words? If so, she hid it well behind a smile. "And I haven't even properly introduced myself. Where are my manners? My name is Maëlle Le Gwenneg."

"Maëlle," he repeated. It felt nice on the tongue. "I'm Talos Tre-Klint."

"I hope to meet you again, Talos."

"If you return to the mountains, you might. I live here," he said, gesturing south along the range towards home before catching himself. What was he doing? If Raffa knew he was showing a human where they lived—hell, if Raffa knew he was talking to a human—his temper would flare. He had no business talking to any humans, not even delicate female ones with sparkling eyes and fascinating pets. He needed to leave.

Almost at a run, he slipped over the edge of the rock ledge and started climbing towards home, stone wings outstretched to help his balance. He heard Maëlle call something behind him, but he didn't look back. If he saw her blue eyes sparkle again, he might not be able to leave.

He was halfway home, the thunderstorm already scattering fat raindrops, when he realized he had left his journal in Maëlle's soft hands.

Chapter Four

Maëlle knelt as still and quiet as she could, but after kneeling on the cold stone floor of the sanctuary for the better part of an hour already, her knees ached. The room was drafty and full of strong incense. And the priestess still droned on with her prayer, blessing Maëlle, cleansing her of spiritual impurity, praying for a fruitful marriage, and whatever else was part of this uncomfortable ceremony.

She wished she had a book to read, though she knew that would be considered rude.

The incense tickled Maëlle's nose. She swallowed her sneeze and tried to distract herself with other thoughts. Like the interesting lithander she had met two days ago.

Finding a giant in the mountains couldn't have surprised her more than running into Talos. Lithander were rare, made rarer by the wars. She knew they generally avoided humans. Books usually described them as cold and feral and dangerous, carved with the teeth and claws of predators.

Talos had been quiet and gentle, not at all the way the histories described them. Tall and slender with the face of a pretty human man and the wings of an eagle, he could almost be mistaken for an angel. She couldn't imagine him picking up a weapon to fight in a war against humans. He had seemed shy, peaceful, curious. He had an artist's eye and attention to detail. She had looked through the journal he left with her several times, tracing his expert sketches with her fingertips as she read his careful notes. A naturalist—and one who did it for the joy of it. Not a warrior.

She had taken to bringing his journal with her everywhere she went so she could return it to him the next time they met. But Gaubert had been keeping her busy with wedding preparations in the two days since. Arwa was sure to be getting lonely in the stables, and Maëlle was beginning to feel a little claustrophobic in the echoing halls of Gaubert's manor.

The priestess, still chanting her prayers, stepped closer to Maëlle in order to daub oil of myrrh on her brow. The strong smell mingled with the incense to make her eyes water. The priestess lifted the bowl of remaining oil heavenward, then dashed its contents across the floor at Maëlle's knees.

If she hadn't been warned about the ceremony ahead of time, Maëlle was sure she would have jumped or cried out at the sudden splash of fragrant oil. As it was, she mostly hid her flinch. Her cold, sore knees were slippery with oil now through the thin fabric of her dress. At least the spilled oil meant the ceremony was almost done. The priestess plucked a blue cornflower from the nearby stems, blessed it, and dropped it in the puddle of oil at Maëlle's knees.

Immediately, the oil turned a red so dark, it may as well be black.

The priestess gasped, stalling in her prayers. A moment later, she started a completely different prayer, one that sounded less like a blessing and more like a plea for help.

"What?" Maëlle asked, despite knowing she was meant to stay quiet. "What does it mean?"

"Do not worry," the priestess said, sounding worried enough herself. "We'll have the midwife examine you."

Several hours later, Maëlle was finally released from the care of the priestess and midwife both. She felt hollow and ached inside, both physically and emotionally. This wasn't how things were supposed to go—how her life was supposed to be. She couldn't decide whether she felt sad or relieved.

She pushed through the door that led to her rooms and found Gaubert waiting for her, sitting in one of the plush chairs in her receiving room, a drink in one hand. Her gut clenched almost painfully.

"That took longer than expected," Gaubert said. He straightened his waistcoat. "Did the priestess have to relearn her prayers from scratch?" The line between his brows screamed anger, despite his calm tone.

Maëlle took a step back. Should she run? Gaubert was clearly in no mood to hear bad news. But it would only be worse if she waited. She swallowed and stepped into her rooms, closing the door quietly behind her.

"I'm barren." She flinched, waiting for his anger. This was what women were meant to do, after all—bear heirs for their husbands. But now, it was a duty that fell beyond her.

"What?"

"Barren. I will never bear children. The priestess learned it during her fertility blessing, and the midwife confirmed it."

"No children." Gaubert stood, glass of whiskey sloshing dangerously in one hand. "No children," he repeated, and this time, there was fire in his words. "No heirs?"

"I'm sorry, Gaubert. It's not something I—" She cut off with a shriek as the glass of whiskey shattered against the wall next to her.

He was across the room in an instant, looming over her, teeth bared. "Women are for heirs and looking pretty. And you're not pretty enough to be a trophy wife."

Maëlle swallowed, trying her best not to back down. "I didn't choose to be barren."

"Worthless woman!" he yelled in her face. "You deceived me. You and your wretched father both."

"You think I knew?" Maëlle was incredulous, floored by the accusation.

"It's your body, woman!"

She felt her own anger rising now, and it took everything she had to keep it from erupting in shouts. "If I was trying to fool you, I would have waited to say anything until after the wedding."

"Lies and deceit," he hissed. "Your cunt is broken. How could you not know?"

Her anger flared too hot to tamp down this time, and she spoke before thinking. "My womb's not on display like some fool's impotence."

The slap hit her solidly on the cheek, sending her staggering backward and into the wall. She stared at Gaubert, at his red face and bared teeth, and the clenched muscles in fists and shoulders. As often as he had made her feel uncomfortable, disparaged her, even yelled at her, he had never before laid a hand on her. The sting was sharp, but the realization was sharper: she wasn't safe here. She had to leave.

"You tell your father," Gaubert said, voice no more than a low rolling growl, "that he's not getting his money back. I need that money—I just don't need you." Then he stormed out of the room, already yelling for the servants to bring him a fresh bottle of whiskey.

As soon as he was gone, Maëlle grabbed her trunk and started to shove her things in it. She would go now before he got drunker and meaner. She grabbed an armful of books, pausing before she could drop them in the chest. But go where? Home was two weeks travel to the north, and her father might just send her back to Gaubert again, holding a receipt for purchase. Or he would send her and a new dowry to the next prospect, who could be even worse. But she had nowhere else to go, no one else to turn to. She had no friends, and the only people she knew here were Gaubert's aunt and servants. And she couldn't stay here, that was clear. Could she take Arwa and hide in the mountains?

The mountains. The image of a pretty face carved in stone. She clutched unconsciously at the journal in her pocket, the one she carried everywhere. Would Talos help her? He had no reason to. Could she even find him?

There was a crash from the other room, the sound of Gaubert's raised voice. Maëlle clenched her jaw and grabbed her riding clothes.

Chapter Five

It was raining, but there was no thunder or lightning, and water was no bother to a lithander. Still, the rain was bad for his journals, so Talos was forced to leave them behind. There would be no bees out today, either. He contented himself with taking his woven grass sunshade from the strawberry patch down to the entrance to his home and patching it there, listening to the rain drum against rock. It was a good rainy-day activity. Maybe, if it was still raining when he finished, he would hunt for new lichens to draw before it got dark.

A screech split the air, echoing between the mountains until it sounded like an animal as large as a bear. Had that been an owl? They didn't normally come out during the day, especially not on rainy days.

He put down his grass sunshade and walked out into the rain, shading his eyes against the falling water for a better view. There may have been something flying high overhead, but he caught only a fluttering glimpse of it. Nothing more. He shrugged, heading back into the wide entryway. He had just sat down with the grass work in his lap when he heard the crunch of rocks on the path, then the scrape of something on the patio. Something large. Frowning, he got up to look outside again and found himself face to face with a gryphon.

Remembering what had happened last time he was so close to a gryphon, he took two steps back, raising an arm in front of his face. But the gryphon didn't lunge at him. It didn't hiss or snap, either. It stood in the rain, dripping and looking miserable until a second form slid from its back.

"Talos?"

He froze, recognizing the voice. "Maëlle?"

He wanted to ask why she was here, why she was in the rain, why she had taken the time to hunt down his home. Having her here was bad, even if she only stayed on the doorstep. But he caught sight of her face under the hood. She was pale and shaking, soaked to the skin. Her blue eyes were big and watery, and he realized she had been crying. He had never seen an animal look so pitiful before. He took her arm and pulled her gently into the entryway, out of the rain. She pulled back her hood, honey-colored hair damp and lank with wet. And he saw her face unobstructed for the first time: cheek red and angry, bruised, with a red cut just at the corner of her mouth. He reached for her, stone fingers gentle on her skin, but she flinched back anyway.

"What happened?" he asked, hand still held in the air between them.

She looked away, eyes filling again with tears. "I...have nowhere to go. It's not safe at home."

So fragile, like a spring flower unused to mountain storms.

"Come in," he said.

It had been a long time since Talos had had a flesh and blood creature in his home—not since Raffa made him get rid of the flying squirrel he had been nursing back to health after a coyote attack. He had forgotten the many things people made of flesh required.

Maëlle had brought nothing with her save the clothes on her back, a saddlebag full of soggy bread and wet apples, and Arwa. Talos brought Arwa into the cave of his home, too, since she didn't seem to like the rain. Maëlle immediately went to the gryphon, snuggling in close under one of her large wet wings.

"I'm sorry to come to you this way," she said, shivering. "Maybe...maybe I should go..."

"You're cold," he said, recognizing the shivers for more than fear.

"Soaked through," she agreed, teeth chattering.

Talos had had a small fire in the hearth, just enough to see by. Lithander didn't need heat the way humans did, though it felt pleasant enough. Seeing Maëlle shivering against the gryphon, he fed the fire new wood until it roared. She took off her soaked cloak and hung it over the back of a chair to drip and dry in the fire's heat. From one pocket, she pulled a bundle of waxed linen, wrapped again and again around a small rectangular shape. She peeled it back carefully, layer after layer, until the book was revealed.

"Your journal," she said, inspecting it for damage before offering it to him. "I was so afraid it would get wet in the rain."

Talos took it, the soft skin of her fingers pliant against his stone. "It's dry," he said, running one hand over the leather cover.

"I'm glad. It would be a shame to ruin such beauty."

"Indeed," he said, watching the way the fire danced in her eyes. "I don't have any food or blankets to offer you. Lithander have no need of either."

"You offered me a roof," she said, and for a moment, that sparkle was there in her eyes. But it fled so quickly he thought he might have imagined it. "That's more than I should have asked for. Thank you, Talos."

He watched Maëlle sleep that night while he mended the sunshade for his strawberries. She slept against Arwa's flank. Her chest rose and fell rhythmically, an occasional soft mewling noise fluttering in her throat. He wondered if she dreamed and, if so, what she dreamed about.

It was so strange having a human here. Such a lesson in contrasts. Talos could choose to rest if he wanted, but he needed no sleep. He didn't breathe, didn't dream. He would not get hot or cold, hungry or thirsty. He was made of stone, after all. Raffa liked to say the lithander were built impervious. Designed to withstand, to outlive and outlast. Raffa talked about sieges in the war and how no one could lay siege like a lithander.

But being a lithander had costs, too. Talos had spent his life watching the social behavior of animals, the packs and hives and mates, the predators and prey. They worked from instinct and for mutual benefit or destruction. Prodded on by hunger or need or fear. It was a beautiful, raw sort of biological clockwork, the way they fit together.

With humans, it was different. They built social connections based on emotions, like no other creature he had witnessed. Humans loved. Talos had read about love, had tried to understand what it meant to humans, how it felt. It was such a foreign concept to him, a lithander who was incapable of love, incapable of relationships, incapable of mating. He had no heart in his stone chest. But he felt a strange yearning to understand nonetheless.

Did Maëlle love, he wondered. And if so, who did she love? And how? Did she love Arwa, the gryphon she leaned into for heat and comfort? Did she love her family? Her friends?

Surely, she couldn't love whoever had bloodied her cheek. Surely not.

Chapter Six

Maëlle woke slowly, nose full of the smell of Arwa's dander and wood smoke, her clothes stiff with dried rain. She loved moments like this. Arwa was warm and soft, and Maëlle could drowse against her forever. For a moment, she thought she was still at home in the north, that she had taken Arwa on an overnight trip into the woods for the sake of quiet or to pick berries, as she had sometimes done in her younger days. But she yawned, and the motion cracked open the cut in the corner of her mouth, and everything came back to her.

There was a crackling sound of fire, a thump of shifting wood. Opening her eyes, she found Talos stoking up the flames. Despite being carved directly into cold stone, the room was pleasantly warm. The firelight danced on Talos's gray surface, highlighting every carefully carved line, tracing every feathered shape. She realized that he wasn't carved with long hair, as she had thought, but with a long flowing mane of feathers, each one so realistic she expected them to be silky under her touch.

Had he kept the fire up all night? It would be for her sake if he had—lithander didn't suffer from the cold. She tried to imagine Gaubert doing the same for her and failed. The thought that this man she had only just met might take such care with her, might change his routine and use his resources after she appeared unasked for and begging on his doorstep, cracked something open inside her. Why did she have to be engaged to a monster like Gaubert and not someone more like Talos? Someone gentle and thoughtful and caring?

She must have made some noise because Talos turned in her direction. "Good morning," he said, his stone wings shifting reflexively behind him. The firelight reflected from his shiny, reddish eyes. Jasper, she thought. Carved carefully and polished to a gleam.

Beneath Maëlle, Arwa stirred and yawned, feathers and fur ruffling and resettling.

"I'm sorry. I had no right to show up at your home last night uninvited." She stood, ignoring the stiffness of her joints. "We'll go."

Talos watched as she collected her dried cloak and ruffled Arwa's neck feathers. She couldn't tell what he was thinking. She realized he was holding one of his journals, a stone finger marking a spot between pages, and wondered if he had been sketching.

"Is your home any safer today than it was last night?" he asked finally, voice quiet.

She froze in the process of adjusting Arwa's saddle straps. Squeezed her eyes shut. Gaubert. Her failure as a woman—as a future wife. That anger and resentment.

"No."

"Do you have somewhere else to go?"

"No."

He shifted, setting the journal down on a nearby chair and coming closer, watching her over Arwa's back. He seemed pensive, unsure—right up until he spoke with conviction. "Then stay."

She expelled a breath of air as if she had been punched. "I...don't want to inconvenience you."

He looked at her bruised cheek, her cut lip. "I don't want you hurt."

Those red eyes, the fall of stone feathers, the flex of granite wings. How could something made of stone look so soft? She bit the inside of her cheek, determined not to cry. Why would he help her? What reason could he have for keeping her safe? She wasn't worth it. But the way he looked at her, open and earnest and a little shy, she couldn't say no.

"Ok," she said, switching to removing Arwa's saddle instead. "I'll stay for now."

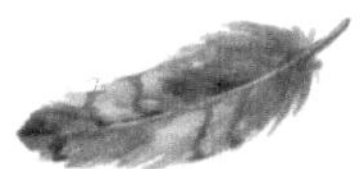

Maëlle only had four apples. The bread was a complete loss, turned to mush by last night's rain. So four apples, and not particularly large ones. She picked one and took a bite, the sweet tang of it waking her stomach into a growl. She hadn't eaten since breakfast the day before and felt hollow now. Was it hunger only? Or was it her newly discovered flaw, too, emptying her out? She pressed a hand to her stomach, feeling—or imagining to feel—the turmoil inside.

She packed her three remaining apples back in the saddlebag until her stomach insisted loudly that one apple was not enough. Two apples now, she reasoned, and she would figure out how to collect more food today. There had to be something she could forage.

She found Talos outside, in the flat, open stone space he called the patio. He had an alpine columbine in a jar of water and was using fine brushes to paint it into one of his journals. His hands were so sure, each line of color precise and perfect.

"I didn't know you paint, too," she said, watching the flower emerge in color on the page.

"I admire color. But it's more difficult to get the details in paint."

"The color is perfect, though." It was true. The rich purple was an exact match, and the bright pops of yellow anthers and vibrant green of leaves set off the whole like the work of art it was.

He paused, his paintbrush hovering over the page. "I'm not as good at painting as sketching."

"You seem a master at both."

Her traitorous stomach chose that moment to growl, and she pressed a fist to her middle with a wince. Talos turned away from his picture to study her.

"You are hungry."

"It's ok," she said. "I know you don't eat. I'll forage for something later."

Talos watched her for a count of five. It should have been unnerving, the way his stone eyes didn't need to blink, but she felt instead as if he was weighing all of her needs and wrapping each in something soft and warm. He dropped his brush into a dish of water, letting the paint bleed away.

"Come with me," he said, rising to his feet.

Maëlle soon realized that Talos was an expert at climbing mountains and cliffs despite his stone weight. He knew exactly where to grasp, exactly how to use his stone wings for balance and counterbalance. He was up the cliff, as spry as a goat, before she had made it a full head's height up.

At least she wore her riding clothes—good boots and leggings under her split skirts—and not the soft shoes and full skirts favored by ladies these days. There was a path of sorts. Maybe that was too generous a word for the narrow goat track that scrabbled up the rock face, but it was better than climbing a sheer cliff. When she was halfway up, Talos peered back over the cliff from above.

"Should I help you?"

Maëlle felt her stubbornness take hold. She set her jaw, gripping tighter to her handhold. "No. I can do it."

He nodded and disappeared back over the cliff top as if he believed her. As if anything she said had to be true. She swallowed back her prepared insistence that she would be fine without help. Swallowed back, too, the bit of fear at her height. She was so used to men insisting on helping her, even when she asked them not to. So used to being treated like she was incapable. She had expected to use her annoyance to fuel the rest of her climb, but instead, Talos had left her to fail or succeed on her own. Had he believed her words? Or did he just not understand how breakable flesh was compared to stone?

At the top, she found something completely unexpected: a garden. Flat sections of clifftop had been layered with soil—he must have carried it up here himself, holding it in place with carefully constructed walls of stone and wood. A rock cistern held water from the previous night's rain, and a sort of woven grass roof provided some shade from the beating sun. An orderly tangle of plants sprawled across the soil surface. Talos knelt at one bed, disentangling a red fruit from the leaves and measuring it with a marked string, writing some notation in one of his copious journals before adding the fruit to a pile he had started nearby.

"Strawberries," she said, awed at the work and care that must go into growing these here, at the top of a mountain, where nothing but rock normally stood.

"Alpine strawberries," Talos agreed. He picked up his small pile of fruits gingerly and held them out to her in cupped hands. He seemed suddenly unsure. Nervous. "Do you like strawberries?"

A laugh bubbled free before she realized it. "I love strawberries."

The ruby fingertip-sized fruits were a special summer treat at home. She would comb the meadows for hours until she had a bowlful, enough for the cook to make jam or pie or cakes, then hours more, plopping the warm fruits in her mouth whole, one at a time, to dissolve like sugared gems on her tongue.

Talos offered his cupped hands to her, closer, and she bit her lip as she chose one. She used her thumbnail to remove the cap and put the whole thing in her mouth, just like she had as a child. She closed her eyes to savor it. It was warmed by the sun and burst with the red taste of sweet summer between her teeth. She let the flavor linger on her tongue before swallowing.

"They're good?" Talos asked.

"Must have been the moan of pleasure that gave it away," she answered, opening her eyes to see his expectant and anxious face smooth to a smile. "I missed the strawberry season this year with the move..." She trailed off, looking unconsciously down the mountains and towards Gaubert's manor.

"Have more," Talos said, lifting his cupped hands to her again. "I have many, and I'm done with these."

"You're sure?"

"I can't eat them," he said with a quirk of a smile. "Someone may as well."

Maëlle let him deposit his handful of berries in her own outstretched hands, then sat on a sun-warmed stone to eat them. She watched Talos work, carefully marking and measuring and making notes. Some of the plants were under woven cages that he tipped back to measure. Others were in the free air, leaves bobbing gently in the breeze. Each plant had a small stick next to it, the top painted with different colors, like they labeled varieties or marked a pattern.

She couldn't hold her curiosity any longer. "What are you doing with your strawberries? If you don't eat them, why grow them?"

"Observations," he said. He peered closer at a leaf, carefully nudging a shiny black beetle from its surface to his stone fingernail. It crawled there while he dug in the bag slung across his shoulder, pulling free a glass lens. It looked like a jeweler's loupe, and he studied the bug through it carefully. "My project this year is all about strawberries—how they grow, their anatomy, the creatures that interact with them."

"And the cages?" she asked, gesturing to the nearest one with the last of her strawberries.

"I wanted to see if pollination leads to bigger fruits. I've been adding bees to some cages and not others." He looked up at her for a moment, perhaps judging her reaction, before rummaging in his bag again. He found a small glass jar, gently brushed the beetle into it, and added a strawberry leaf before corking it shut.

Maëlle got up and looked closely inside one of the cages, checking each of the creamy white flowers for movement. "Are there bees in here now?" she asked, looking in a second cage.

"No. I let them go when they're done. I don't want to trap them away from their hive. I don't want to hurt them."

She looked up, surprised. He was worried about bees. What kind of man worried about bees? It made her heart swell. Talos had such a gentle way, such soft attentiveness. Such sweetness from this stone creature.

"You know," she said carefully, wanting to offer him some prize in return for his jewel-like strawberries, "I read a lot of books."

He smiled at her, and she remembered she had been reading a book the first time they met.

"All kinds of books. In one of those books, I read about pollinating strawberries by hand."

"By hand?" He looked at his blunt-tipped stone fingers. "I'm not sure my hands would do the job."

"With a brush," she clarified. "A small paint brush, like the one you were using to paint the columbine, but clean and dry. The bristles can pick up pollen from one flower and deposit it on the...the female part of another flower."

"The stigma," Talos supplied. "The top of the pistil." He tapped his chin in thought. "It doesn't hurt the flower?"

Hurt the flower? Oh, sweet lord, her chest ached.

"No more than a pollinator. It's time- and labor-intensive, but..." She looked at the cages again. "So is catching and releasing bees, I suspect."

Talos looked at his bed of flowers, at the cages, at the berries. Then he strode to Maëlle and took her hands in his. She was surprised by the warmth and smoothness of the stone against her skin. His touch was so infinitely delicate, as if she were made of glass, and he feared shattering her. And yet, he held her hands in his and gave her all the earnestness those jasper-red eyes of his could hold.

"Will you show me how?" he asked.

And she couldn't stand to tell him that she had never done it before. That she had only read about it and seen a couple of rudimentary sketches of the process. That she had never even grown a plant before in her life. It was all she could do not to lift his hands to her lips and kiss their tenderness, a benediction for the stone man who worried about hurting bees and flowers, who worried about hurting her. She settled instead for a smile, hoping she could put as much warmth in the expression as she felt beating and building behind her ribs.

"Of course," she said.

Chapter Seven

Talos made a habit of bringing Maëlle strawberries every morning. It was his favorite time of day; her eyes would go that sparkly blue of happiness, the same he had noted on their first meeting—like sunlight on a deep glacial pool.

Blue was quickly becoming his favorite color.

He would climb to the cliff early in the day, sometimes even before the sun came up, to make sure the berries were waiting when she woke. Sometimes, Arwa would join him, lying on the rocks around the garden and napping in the morning mist. It was strange, not to be alone most of the time. Arwa made excellent company, mostly quiet but a warm presence nonetheless. Maëlle made for even better company. He enjoyed talking with her the way he had never been able to talk with Raffa. She was fascinated by his journals, enamored with his art. She spoke of books she had read, adding to his knowledge from her memory. They often sat long into the night in front of the fire in quiet conversation.

Several days after her arrival, as he was finishing his measurements and about to carry his cache of picked strawberries to Maëlle, he heard an unexpected sound. He paused, hands full of berries. The sound, as clear as trilling birdsong, rose and fell and echoed around the cliffs of the mountains like crystalline beams of light through a faceted gem.

He thought it must be some creature he had never seen before. A caladrius, maybe, or a golden phoenix. Did the alkonost live this far west? Then he saw Arwa circle through the air to land on the stone patio below the way she always did when following the call of her master, and he realized the song came from inside his home.

Entranced, he climbed down from his perch, half-full basket of berries forgotten. The music came clearer here, and he could make out words with it. A sad, sweet song of love and loss that shivered in the air like pure struck silver. It had to be Maëlle singing, didn't it? Who else was there to sing in his home?

Talos ran a hand along Arwa's back as he passed, and she huffed a soft breath of air against his cheek, folding her front paws to lay in the sun and listen. He felt drawn to go farther, though. To hear the music closer. To see Maëlle's face as she sang. There was sadness in the music but beauty, too—much like Maëlle herself.

She was by the fire, running a wooden comb through her honey-gold hair and watching the flames dance. The way her rockrose-colored lips shaped sound, the dip and stretch of her throat, the way her chest swelled and shrank with air... It was enchanting to watch, this ephemeral and fragile being creating ephemeral and fragile music. The firelight made Maëlle look aglow. Her hair fell around her like spun sunlight. She held her eyes closed as she rocked with the music.

Talos had never seen anything look so alive before.

In the song, a faerie prince danced with a human maiden and fell in love, only to lose her at dawn light, when the connection between their two worlds dissolved. The words were sad, but the melody was what struck the chord. Talos had no heart, but he felt the heartache of the song anyway, the way it shimmered over his surface, like being struck by a tuning fork vibrating in the key of pure melancholy.

What was this magic? How could one woman's voice, one song of pure fancy, build in him the illusion of emotion? How was it that whatever he held inside his lithander body—soul or animas magic or something else—could echo back with it? Lithander didn't form relationships and were incapable of love, but with nothing more than vibrations in the air and a few metered words, Maëlle made him feel like maybe he could understand it. Someday. Maybe today.

He felt dizzy with it. He had to press a hand to the wall to keep from swaying, to keep from staggering. The sound of stone on stone was enough to catch Maëlle's attention. Her song cut off abruptly, with a hand to her mouth in surprise and something that could be shame. He felt hollowed out with the music gone. Empty and aching.

"I'm sorry," Maëlle said around the hand pressed to her lips. "I didn't mean to disturb you."

Disturb him? Only in the way it stirred him up inside. Only in the way it made him feel alive. He found one of his hands at his breast, fingers clenching against granite as if he could carve himself out from the inside and offer the contents to her on a palm.

"Don't...don't stop," he managed.

That pink blush of spring beauties was on her cheeks again. "What?"

"Please. Don't stop singing, Maëlle. I want to hear the end of the song."

She blinked at him, eyes large and unsure. "You...want to?"

He strode across the room to take her hand in his, to uncover her mouth. He held her flesh as gently as a bee. As gently as a flower petal. "More than anything."

She studied him, lips slightly parted. Then she looked away, taking her hand back from his grasp. "Father always chided me for singing. Women should not make so much noise, he says. Gaubert..." She paused, swallowing hard, and Talos wondered who this man was who made Maëlle so sad and fearful. Was he the one who had left the fading bruise on her cheek? "Gaubert calls it squawking. Women should be seen and not heard."

He couldn't stand the sadness lacing her words, the way she looked at the floor and closed down her expression with a vice of shame.

"No. That can't be right."

She turned to look at him, tentative but with the faintest gleam of hope gilding her eyes. There were tears caught in her lower lashes, sparkling like diamonds, and he couldn't resist the urge to brush them aside with a thumb.

"How could nature give you a voice like yours and ask you not to use it? It would be like asking the passionflower not to bloom or asking the sunset not to glow." His stone palm rested against her bruised cheek as lightly as a butterfly on a flower. Her skin was warm, soft hairs as fine as down. Her breath hitched. She trembled slightly, and he worried his touch hurt the healing bruise there, but she leaned into his palm. "Will you finish your song? For me?"

She closed her eyes, biting her lower lip. "No one has ever asked me to sing before." When she opened her eyes again, they were sparkling more than he had ever seen, the blue deeper than seemed possible.

Talos would ask her every day, morning and night, if it meant that happiness would dance in her eyes.

She stepped back, breaking contact with his touch. But she didn't look away this time. Her blue eyes held his like she was giving him the gift of her confidence along with the sweet melody. She licked her lips, and with a breath that drew in air like sunshine, she continued her song.

In the lyrics, the faerie prince, shattered by losing his human love, foreswore his kingdom and crown, foreswore the faerie people, foreswore the font of magic, and was banished to the mortal realm. There, he found his love, but she had aged while he was in faerie still. An old woman on her deathbed. And still, the faerie prince loved her, and she him. He held her, and when he kissed her, he gave her the last of his magic. It was enough to peel back the years and leave her as young as when they first danced. But without his magic, the prince would now age and die the same as a mortal, in time with his love.

It should be a bittersweet ending, wrapped up with the bittersweet melody from Maëlle's lips. But it struck something in Talos that shouldn't be struck. His chest was aching again, though there was no reason for it. He pressed a palm there. Maybe he could push the ache back inside if he pressed hard enough.

Maëlle watched him as she sang the end of the song, eyes lingering on the hand at his breast. She looked afire, with the flush in her cheeks and the halo of golden hair, lit by the flames in the hearth behind her. She was still a thing of flesh and blood and bone, still breakable and mortal, but she looked stronger than he had ever seen. Standing tall, eyes unwavering on his, voice a clarion call through the morning air. There was something of magic in this woman, Talos thought. Surely this wasn't just a woman, a human with mundane human emotions. She felt like so much more.

The last notes of the song echoed between the rock walls of his home, leaving the residue of memory on every surface they touched. Talos didn't need to breathe but still somehow felt out of breath. "Beautiful," he gasped. He wanted to add that it was heartbreaking, but it felt wrong to say such things when he had no heart.

Maëlle gave a small smile, once again demure. She tucked a loose wisp of honeyed hair behind an ear, the motion as delicate as dawn light. "Thank you for listening."

She hesitated, then stepped forward to press her hand against his where he held it against his chest. It was the first time she had reached out to touch him, and she pressed more firmly than he expected. Warm and soft, but strong too. How had he not noticed before, the way she stood up to the world?

"Thank you for everything, Talos."

Something that was not quite a shiver ran through him at the vulnerability laid bare in her gaze. He couldn't imagine how she kept from bruising herself on the world with every touch.

Chapter Eight

Maëlle sat near Talos on the stone patio, reclining against Arwa's side and reading one of his journals about trees in the Rochesne Mountains. He was painting again—this time a picture of Arwa. He had been working on his entry on owl gryphons for his naturalist journals. Yesterday, he'd shown her some of the sketches so far, and Maëlle had been speechless at their beauty. It didn't matter whether it was a full-body sketch of Arwa in flight or a detailed study of one of her flight feathers, the precision and form were exquisite.

She had never enjoyed so many quiet moments with someone else before, not the way she had since coming to Talos's home. They talked about nature and art, but they also spent hours like now, each in quiet contemplation of their own pursuit while sharing space with each other. It felt so good, so natural, that she had to remind herself that coming here hadn't solved her problems. Gaubert was still out there, no doubt still angry, and she was still engaged to marry him. She was and always would be barren, a failure as a woman. And the wedding was planned for...

She counted the days in her head and grimaced. So soon. What would happen if she just didn't return? If she ran away and never came back? She could take Arwa over the mountains and keep going, find a little cottage for herself somewhere, and live alone. Once, the idea would have drawn her; so often, she had preferred no company over that of her companions. But now?

She entertained a moment's fancy of what it would be like to stay here with Talos forever, sharing moments of gentle quiet and pleasant conversation. And those other moments, too—the ones of pure and shocking grace. The sharing of strawberries. The worry for bees. The pleading for song.

She watched Talos move his brush smoothly over the paper, as delicate as an evening breeze. She couldn't ask it of him, of course. And he had no reason to let her stay anyway.

Lithander and humans were not allies, let alone friends. And she knew she was a burden, needing food and water and heat and more that he had no use for otherwise.

He looked up, perhaps sensing the weight of her eyes on him. "You look sad," he said.

"Melancholy, maybe."

Those jasper red eyes watched her like he could read an entire story in her expression. Finally, he dropped his brush in the nearby cup, turning the water blue with paint. "I'd like to take you somewhere," he said. It was tentative, almost a question, but ribboned through with hope. Maëlle felt the strange urge to brush fingertips along the carved feathers of his mane and brush away his hesitancy with no more than a touch.

"I'll get my cloak," she said.

Maëlle rode Arwa while Talos climbed below. It was obvious from how he moved that he knew every inch of these mountains, knew exactly where to step or grasp or jump to get where he was going. She admired his confidence, even if it was born of knowing he wouldn't be hurt in a fall. She admired, too, the graceful arch of his wings as he spread or shifted them for balance. The feathers there were carved every bit as intricately as the ones in his mane, but they were shot through with white veins in the gray stone. Whatever the white stone was, it sometimes caught the light and glittered in the sun.

He led her through a steep crevasse between two mountains clogged with rock falls and the skeletons of fallen spruces. It was cooler at these heights, and the tops of the mountains were still white with snow. There was so much barren rock, painted with pale lichen and nothing more. It seemed a bleak and desolate place.

The way narrowed as they went, and Arwa had to circle higher to avoid clipping her wings against the rock walls. Maëlle tugged her cloak tighter around herself, the wind blowing chill off the snow and ice of the mountain caps. And it was at those greater heights that she caught the first glimpse of deep, shining blue, so out of place in the colorless landscape.

They burst into the valley from on high, well before Talos arrived, and the view below spread out as pristine and clear as a dream. A lake filled with impossible, bottomless blue. At one end of the valley, a wall of blue ice nosed up to the lake, leaving drifting pieces of white ice floating on its surface. With the breeze rippling the waters and the sun on high, the lake glittered like a million flawless sapphires, and Maëlle couldn't breathe at the beauty of it.

Arwa circled the lake once, lazily, while Maëlle caught her breath. They flew over the surface, close enough to brush the water with Arwa's back talons. Maëlle watched their reflection on the surface as they flew, the image as sparkling and depthless as the waters.

When they came back around, Talos was there, among a stand of spruce and alder, standing atop a flat rock the size of her father's dining room table, his bag open in his hands, watching her and Arwa soar. He was too far away to know for sure, but she would have sworn he was smiling—that hesitant, gentle smile of his. The one that seemed too human for a stone face.

She coaxed Arwa to the ground in a flat scrabble of rock by the lake and left her to chase fish in the shallows while she walked back to Talos. He was sitting now, long legs stretched forward. He had spread a cloth on the stone—where had he gotten a cloth?—and set it with a sampling of foods. Strawberries from his garden, but also watercress and chickweed, acorns and chestnuts, burdock root and wild onions, blueberries and bunchberries and cranberries and cloudberries—the foods he had taught her to forage to keep herself fed. And next to them, on a shallow dish carved of stone, was a piece of honeycomb fragrant with honey and dotted with fresh violets.

"Honey," she gasped, kneeling on the rock at the cloth's edge. She reached out one finger until it just brushed the golden liquid, holding the drop on her fingertip. It glowed like amber in the sunlight. "Where did you find honey?"

"From a beehive."

"Obviously," she said with a laugh.

"It's not like bees can sting me."

"No, I suppose not." But she was thinking more about his concern for the bees in his garden when he had been unwilling to hurt them for the sake of his strawberries. Talos shifted, wrapping one arm around himself as if hearing her thoughts.

"A bear found the hive first. This piece was broken and abandoned by the bees."

She smiled. There he was, the gentle lithander. He had probably tried to repair the hive as much as he could before taking the honey. She sucked the honey from the tip of her finger, letting the sweet dissolve into her mouth and down her throat.

"You brought me a picnic," she said, shaking her head. "A feast. I could have carried this in Arwa's saddlebags, Talos. You did not need to carry so much for me."

He shrugged. "I wanted to."

And how could she argue with that?

"And this place?" she asked, surveying the view of the crystalline lake cupped in hands of tall stone ridges and dark green foliage.

"It's a glacial lake." He pointed across the lake at the blue ice by the water. "The glacier helps feed it now, but it's deep. Long ago, the glacial ice filled this whole space, wedging its way down into the rock. When it melted, it became this lake."

"It's beautiful." The sunlight dazzled her, the blue so rich it made her dizzy.

Talos shifted, turning to watch her survey the scene. "It's the exact color of your eyes," he said so quietly she almost didn't hear.

"Oh." Maëlle wasn't sure what else to say, but her stomach fluttered the same way it did when she rode Arwa into a free fall. Blue like a glacial lake—such poetry. She needed something to distract her from the blush on her cheeks. And look, Talos had provided her with an array of tasty distractions. She took a strawberry first because she loved them and because Talos had grown them himself and because eating them always felt like an exchange of gifts.

"What do they taste like?" Talos asked.

She turned to find him watching her with his steady observer's gaze. "Strawberries?"

"Yes. I've never tasted them—never tasted anything."

She mulled over her answer as she slowly chewed another berry for inspiration. How could she describe the joy and sweetness and tang of fruit to someone who couldn't eat, couldn't taste, couldn't smell?

"They taste like...one of those summer afternoons when the light is long, the air is heavy, and the meadows are full of flowers and bees, and you know that this moment is rare and brief, but it's all the sweeter for it. If you could take an afternoon like that and find its warm heart and hold it in your hand, warm as glowing amber... That's what they taste like."

Talos picked up one of the fingertip-sized red berries, looking at it more closely. "You make taste sound like a journey."

"Every experience in life is a journey if you take the time to notice it."

He smiled at her then, brightly and with more than his usual quirk of lips, and Maëlle felt warm and clear and shimmery inside. She had never felt so happy, so content before in her life.

"Maybe I'll grow strawberries again next year," Talos said, voice distracted and thoughtful and fuzzed with hesitancy. His jasper red eyes looked from his strawberry to her and back, as shy as a butterfly.

Something inside her cracked and rang like a shattering crystal goblet. Next year. Next year, she would be married to Gaubert unless he packed her home to her father instead. Next year, she would be under someone's thumb regardless. And she still wouldn't—never would—be with child. It was a gift she could give no one. She felt hollow again, despite the strawberries in her stomach—hollow and untethered. She may as well be looking at a dream through the tarnished silver of an old and cloudy mirror.

"Maëlle," he said. He reached a hand as gentle as a bird and brushed her chin to turn her face towards him. "What is it that makes you so sad?"

How? How could someone made of stone be so soft? She wanted to shatter under his fragility, his care, until she came apart into a hundred million pieces of light. Instead, she brushed tears from her eyes with the back of her hand and forced a smile.

"I'm engaged to be married, Talos. In only a couple days' time."

His fingertips rested still on her chin, warm and light, barely a touch at all. "Married." He let his hand fall.

"It's an arranged marriage. Gaubert Desroches."

For a moment, he studied the waters, the way sunlight laughed on their surface. "You love him?"

Maëlle gave a laugh that was half sob, and Talos turned back to study her again. "Talos." She said his name as a sigh, one knitted from sadness. "Arranged marriages are not made for love. It's my obligation. Gaubert is my father's choice, not mine."

He didn't understand. She saw it in the arch of his brow and the brief part of lips, the jasper red eyes drawn down. Marriage was a complicated enough topic for a lithander to grasp—they had no marriage of their own, she knew. But this must seem as strange as the faeries to him—an arranged marriage, not for love but for profit. The duties of family. It confused her, too, truth be told. The ways of the human world were clearly not easy to grasp.

Talos reached out a hand again, hesitant this time. When she didn't flinch away, didn't turn from his gaze, he brushed a petal-soft thumb over her cheek, tracing her fading bruise. "Was this Gaubert the one who hurt you?"

The ache in her chest threatened to swallow her whole. She didn't answer—couldn't answer—and knew that would be answer enough. She saw when he understood, the way his eyes stilled and his jaw set, and the concern bloomed large over his whole face. But his hand lingered still at her cheek, cupped there like he could shield her from any further blows, any further hurt. She couldn't stand it. Any longer, and she would break. So she reached up to take his hand in both of hers, gently held it, and brought it to her lips to kiss the stone of his knuckles.

When she looked up from his hand, she realized Talos's eyes had gone wide. Not in fear, not in displeasure, not in shock. She could tell he was surprised, but the curve of his parted lips was the shape of pleasure writ large. The sight spread warmth through her chest, a balm against the ache. She couldn't help herself; she kissed his hand once more, enjoying the subtle reactions on Talos's face as she did: a flutter of stone lashes, a tremble of lips, eyes focused on her like she was the world.

The books gave the lithander too little credit, she realized. They may not have a flesh and blood heart, but they were clearly capable of emotional depth. She thought that if she stared into those jasper eyes of his for too long, she might drown in that emotional depth.

She refused to look away.

"Maëlle," he whispered. His fingers clenched in her grip reflexively, and she let his hand go. It stayed between them like a fluttering bird. "Maëlle," he said again. His words were so soft, the distant sounds of shifting ice almost drowned them out completely. "I think I would like to kiss you properly."

"Properly?" She couldn't breathe, couldn't move, but she found a smile for him anyway. "It would be proper to ask first, then."

She half expected he wouldn't, that he would balk at the idea of kissing and emotions with a human. But his gaze, steady as the stone he was carved from, never left hers.

"May I try to kiss you, Maëlle?"

A piece of her heart broke loose and fluttered up into her throat. "Only try?" she managed, trying to keep her tone light.

"Well," he said, then paused. Considered. "I've never kissed someone before. I might not do it right."

Oh, sweet lord, his expression—earnest and simple and shy, every shade of gentle, and so very much him. The air was thick with the smell of honey and strawberries, the sunlight pouring in like sapphires and gold. If she could bottle this moment for later, keep it in a locket around her neck forever, she could endure anything.

"I'm sure you'll do it right," she said, voice caught to breaking.

"Is that a yes?"

"Yes, Talos. That's a yes."

He slid closer, close enough for her to see the individual black and white and gray grains in the granite of his lips. She felt drawn to him, like he had charmed gravity into pulling her closer. His hand, the one she had kissed, slid around her neck and up under her hair. His touch was warm, always warmer than she expected of stone, and the texture of granite on her nape set her skin humming. The moment felt as large as the world, as full as the ocean, as long as time itself, everything shivering on the brink of *something*.

And when he leaned forward the last few inches, his lips were hot on hers—like kissing the sun. Stone should be hard, ungiving, but as she gasped and leaned into the kiss, she felt his mouth go soft under hers, like warmed and worked clay. None of the books mentioned anything like this.

He made a small noise, one that could be a whimper or a groan. She worried that it was uncomfortable for him, the transition to pliability. But if it was, he ignored it. The hand on the back of her neck pressed her forward, closer to Talos, into his kiss until she thought he would melt under her, and she would melt with him, and they would pour together into the lake to live forever entwined in those blue glacial waters.

Chapter Nine

Talos was melting, and he didn't care.

Maëlle's lips were as soft as velvet lichen, soft as flower petals, and warm too. He was afraid he would bruise her, stone as he was—that he might hurt her. Was afraid that the immense heat building inside him would scald her skin. But she leaned into him, unafraid, like she could breathe him in. Maybe she wasn't as fragile as he thought.

But the heat—why did he feel melted inside? He thought at first it was Maëlle's, that her warm-blooded body was radiating into him. And he could feel the warmth of her in the few inches of air between their bodies, an invisible halo of heat around her. But the heat in him was something different. It was more, hotter, brighter. He must be completely molten inside. Crack him open like an egg, and he was sure he'd spill a flood of lava.

And it was changing him—softening him—like wax too near the fire. His lips went soft, and his fingertips on Maëlle's neck and his knee where it rested against hers. Anywhere he touched her, he felt himself become tender. He didn't know this could happen to lithander, had never heard of it happening before. It should scare him. It should make him pull back from the kiss and make sure he wasn't damaged. But it felt so *good*, achingly good, and he leaned into it instead, leaned into Maëlle, a man built of hunger instead of granite.

Was this how kissing a woman felt to humans? How did they stand it? How did they not go blind or deaf or dumb with it? How did they not combust or disintegrate or shatter?

How did they not do it every minute of every day?

The heat, as heavy and rich as magma, stayed in his chest. It stayed when the kiss ended. It stayed when he and Maëlle finally packed up the picnic in the fading light of day. It stayed as they traveled home again in the half-dark, and every time he caught sight of her on Arwa's back above, it pulsed hotter and richer. And when they were home, when the fire was stoked, when

Talos was staring into the flames and trying to find answers in their depths, when Maëlle climbed into his lap and fell asleep with her tender cheek against his stone chest, the heat nested like a permanent thing inside him.

Maëlle thrummed with the evidence of life: chest rising and falling, heart beating, closed eyelids fluttering. He felt like he was holding infinite possibility in his lap. His lips had resolidified when the kiss was done, and his fingertips and knee, too. But now, the arm he had wrapped around her sleeping form had gone soft as clay, and his lap had done the same. He could feel the curled shell of Maëlle's ear imprinting in the soft spot on his chest, right over where a human's heart would be.

What was happening to him? Why was he so soft around this woman? He ached inside with three parts pleasure and one part pain, and rock should feel neither. Was he broken somehow? Would he fall apart? How long would this feeling last? If he kept Maëlle close, would he feel this way forever?

It was an experiment he couldn't carry out—not with her engaged to be married and Raffa due home in a few days. A flight of fancy, he thought. Something to pass the time while he watched Maëlle sleep. Would it be improper to kiss her forehead while she slept? He gently brushed a wisp of hair from her cheek and hoped she wasn't too uncomfortable. He couldn't bring himself to move her, not when she had willingly curled herself against him.

Maëlle was engaged to a man who hurt her. Talos didn't want her hurt—but it wasn't his choice. He had nothing to offer

Maëlle, nothing he could use to keep her away from Gaubert. He was heartless and couldn't love her. Even Gaubert, human as he was, had the capacity for love. Talos couldn't even offer Maëlle permanent sanctuary. Raffa wouldn't stand for it. Raffa, who had a son to carve, who thought the lithander people needed the numbers to defend themselves from people of flesh, who thought humans were weak and inferior, short-lived and cruel. If Raffa knew Talos had a human woman here in their home...

Just before dawn, the sound of Arwa hissing outside on the patio brought Talos back to alertness. Lithander didn't need sleep, but he had been enjoying drowsing against Maëlle while she slept, and time had slipped past unnoticed. The fire in the hearth had half burned down, though Maëlle was warm in his arms, golden hair curtaining her sleeping features. He should put more wood on the fire. He didn't want it to get too cold in here for Maëlle's sake, and stone walls tended to eat the heat. But it felt impossible to move Maëlle from his lap, asleep as she was. Surely he would wake her. Her rockrose-colored lips were parted slightly, letting the breath of sleep escape. He remembered what it felt like to press his own lips against hers, stoking the heat in his chest.

Outside, Arwa screeched. Talos frowned, looking towards the door. Gryphons were mostly diurnal, sleeping during the night and hunting during the day. It was strange for Arwa to be hunting before the sun was up. Was there an animal outside? A raccoon? Or something bigger—a bear or cougar, maybe?

He heard a returning growl from farther out and froze. He knew that sound—the animal ferocity, the stubbornness, the resonant stone chest.

Raffa.

Panic made the heat in Talos's chest pucker up and twist into knots. Raffa shouldn't be home for another couple days yet. Talos heard Raffa shout again and knew he wasn't imagining it—it was his brother. Talos shifted Maëlle gently to a place on the floor, folding her cloak under her head as a pillow. She stirred and mumbled something in her sleep, but her eyes stayed closed.

Raffa had chased Arwa into flight, and the owl gryphon circled overhead with plaintive screeches. The bear-sized lithander growled back, hands clenched to fists so the claws were extended from his knuckles. In the almost-dark of predawn, Raffa's eyes looked less like black flint and more like gaping wounds in his face.

"Raffa," Talos said, trying to bring his brother's attention away from Arwa.

"What's that beast doing on the patio?" Raffa asked, scowling at the gryphon overhead. "Don't tell me you adopted another pet while I was gone."

"She's not mine."

"Wretched creature."

Beyond Raffa, the cart loomed in the dim light, left where Raffa had dropped the yoke in the gravel. An imposing shape filled most of the cart's bed, larger than Talos had expected. The block of granite was covered with a canvas tarp and tied down with thick ropes; the cart sagged under its weight.

"You're home earlier than expected," Talos said.

Raffa made one more growling noise, waving his arms menacingly in Arwa's direction before turning a tired gaze on Talos. "Anxious to get started." Started on carving. On his son. Raffa would want to set up by the light of the fire immediately. The image of Maëlle sleeping by the fire, right where Raffa would want to stand his granite, filled him with momentary fear.

"Raffa, I need to tell you something."

"Help me unload this first, will you? It's damn heavy."

"This is important."

"And I'm tired. Come on, you can talk while we untie it, at least."

"There's a woman inside our home."

Raffa went still, looking at Talos with his gaping hole eyes. "A *human* woman?"

"She's not like you think."

Raffa flexed his hands, bringing out his knuckle claws. His teeth ground together like fault lines, granite on granite. "You let a human into our home?"

"She was hurt and had nowhere else to go."

"Dammit, Talos!" Raffa turned and punched the rock wall, leaving gouges in its surface. "This is like that flying squirrel all over again, only ten times worse. You have a softer heart than most humans, and you don't even *have* a heart." He paced down the length of the wagon, turning abruptly to come back and wave a finger under Talos's nose. "You can't keep her."

Talos frowned back, crossing his arms against his brother's anger. "She's not a pet. She's a person."

"And what the hell are you going to do with a human person?"

If Talos could blush, he would have then. Certainly, the warmth inside was rekindled, flaring as hot as before, when he was kissing or holding Maëlle. "Take care of her. Keep her safe." Make her eyes sparkle with happiness, he didn't say. Feed her sweet summer fruit. Maybe kiss her again by blue glacial waters.

Raffa let out a harsh laugh. "That sounds a lot like a pet, brother."

"She's not a pet!" Talos was surprised by the volume of his own voice, the way it echoed off stone and rang into the air. His wings twitched in irritation, his hands clenching and unclenching in fists. "She's a person—someone with fears and loves and challenges, opinions and goals. She's a woman, one with honey-gold hair and blue eyes the color of a glacial lake and a smile as warm as sunshine. One that loves strawberries and sings sad faerie songs and reads my journals like they're more than just silly—"

He cut off abruptly, knowing Raffa wouldn't understand, that this wasn't the way to make him understand. But it was too late. Raffa was already looking at him with lip curled and shoulders tensed and eyes like black holes. The disdain in his stare was filled with the ghost of every human he had fought during the last war.

"Pretty words about this woman," Raffa said. His voice had lost its anger, settling instead into a much more frightening, deadly chill. "Do you think you can keep her the way a human husband would?"

"No, you don't—"

Raffa cut him off with a finger to the chest. "You can't. Lithander don't marry because we don't love, Talos. If you keep her, it would be as a captive or a pet. You can't love her."

"There's more to it than—"

Raffa poked him again. "You can't love her, and you can't give her a child." Another finger prod. "Humans are all obsessed with sex and love and reproduction, and you can give her none of that." An open-palmed shove this time, and it felt like it came with a breaking in Talos's chest. "Whatever you may think, you are not good for her, Talos. And she's not good for you, either. I don't care how...blue her eyes are or whatever else you're fixated on." Raffa threw his hands in the air. "Dammit, you brought a *human* into our *home*! Why did you think that was a good idea? How could this end any way but bad?"

Talos wanted to argue with his brother, but everything he said was true. The knowledge settled like a hunk of iron in his chest, dense and heavy and sluggish. Why would Maëlle even want to stay with him when he had so little to offer her? Nothing in the way of physical comforts or any true emotional bond. No hope of children or marriage. He barely had the necessities to keep her alive—heat and space and food—and those would get harder with winter. The strawberries would die back in the fall, and she couldn't eat his sketches.

But there was that memory of Maëlle on his doorstep, drenched in rain, half in tears, cheek bruised and lip bleeding. Of Maëlle hurting and not knowing where else to go. Of Maëlle saying it was unsafe at home.

"You have to get rid of her," Raffa said, voice gentler now. "You know she can't stay."

"She's not safe at home."

"Then that's a problem for humans to solve. Not you."

"You don't care that she's in danger."

"No, I don't. It's not our problem. It's not *your* problem."

"You hate humans so much," Talos said, but even though his words were laced with bitterness, they sounded hollow and feeble, like the shed exoskeleton of a cicada.

Raffa sighed, placing a hand on Talos's shoulder. "I do hate humans, yes. But I only want what's best for you, brother."

Talos felt fragile and lost. "I know you do," he agreed. But even he didn't know what was best for him, and there was still a woman in their home.

Chapter Ten

He found Maëlle up by the strawberry patch. He hadn't heard her wake and hadn't heard her climb, but when he didn't find her in front of the fire, it was the first place he looked. She was on a rock, knees drawn up and hugged to her chest, watching the sunrise tickle the horizon. Her honey-colored hair was tousled still with sleep, and she held one of Talos's journals pressed between her knees and chest. She looked fragile again, the way she had seemed when Talos first saw her—small and soft and ephemeral, something that could be bruised too easily. The spring flower, unused to harsh winds.

Talos felt the irrational urge to wrap her up in his arms, to pull her back into his lap and curl around her like a protective shell. Instead, he sat on the rock near her and watched the sun crest the horizon with a bloody wash of red light. The harsh color made her almost-healed bruise stand out again, stark against her pale cheek.

"Maëlle," he said finally, then found he wasn't sure what to say next. His stone wings shifted in discomfort. It had been so much easier yesterday—everything had been so much easier.

"I heard your conversation with Raffa," she said, not turning away from the crimson sunrise.

"He's my brother," Talos said, trying to explain. "We were carved by the same father."

"He doesn't want me here."

Talos watched her breathing in the morning air, chest rising and falling. He watched her tighten her grip around her knees until the knuckles went white. He watched her not look at him, not even when her hair brushed her face in the mild morning breeze.

"He was carved for war," Talos said, closing his eyes. "His whole life has been hating humans."

"You care about him." Her words were soft, and when Talos opened his eyes, he found she was watching him instead of the sunrise now, her cheek resting on top of her knees.

"I do. We take care of each other."

She gave a smile then, but it wasn't the kind that made her eyes sparkle. Rather, it was a sad smile, the same kind she used when singing one of her tragic faerie songs. It struck Talos like a tuning fork, the melancholy echoing through him in resonance.

"I'm glad," she said, and he could tell she meant it. She sat up then, eyes reflecting the red sky like they were burning with something desperately important. "But he's wrong."

"Wrong," Talos repeated. "About what?"

"A lot of what he said. But most importantly, he was wrong that lithander can't love."

"Maëlle…" Her name burned him on the way out, and he had to pause to let the pain dissipate before continuing. "He's not wrong, not about that. It's…a law of nature. Lithander can't love."

"Can you feel happiness, Talos?"

"Of course."

"And sadness?"

"Yes," he said, more hesitant this time because he was starting to see the shape of her argument. It was a path he had foolishly followed himself before, as a younger lithander, in hopes of discovering some new truth.

"Anger? Fear? Hate? Curiosity? Pleasure? Disappointment?"

Talos drew his own knees up to his chest, wanting to press the leaden feeling in his chest until it ached less. "I understand your line of reasoning, Maëlle. I do. But those other emotions aren't the same as love. Just because we feel some emotions doesn't mean we feel all emotions."

"Why? What makes love different?"

She asked it earnestly, but also like the question contained the entire shape of the world. Her rockrose-colored lips were slightly parted, her breath fogging into the chill morning air. Every hair on her body shone pink in the light of sunrise, right down to the fine hairs that fuzzed her face and neck. The effect was enchanting, setting her aglow with the pink of life. Talos wanted to run his fingertips across her skin and collect that pink, put it in a jar to paint with later. His hand was halfway to her before he stopped himself. Instead, he pressed two fingers to her chest, just over her heart. He felt its gentle rhythm through her skin.

"This," he said. He pulled his hand back and rapped a knuckle against his own solid chest. "Lithander don't have a heart."

"So?"

He stared at her. "How can we love when we have no heart?"

She sighed and reached out to take his hand, warming it between the two of hers. "Talos, love doesn't live in the heart." He couldn't take his eyes off the way his gray stone hand looked between her two soft, pink ones. Already, he felt his fingers and palms going soft at her touch, felt the fire inside him roar higher, even as he felt like he was falling off a tall cliff. "We—hu-mans—say love is an emotion of the heart because we feel it here." She pressed his hand and both of hers to his breast. "But that's just a physiological response. Racing heart. Faster breathing. Fluttering or tightness or chills."

"Heat?" Talos asked, overwhelmed by the heat in his own chest.

"Yes, heat sometimes, too. But the heart doesn't cause love."

It sounded lovely—like a fairytale. One of Maëlle's faerie songs, where love could conquer all, even if there was heartache as well. But it couldn't be true.

He pulled their hands away from his chest, disengaging from Maëlle's warm touch. "No, I've read human books. They all say love comes from the heart."

"It's a metaphor, Talos. Poetry." And it was clear she saw in his gaze that he didn't believe her by the press of her lips and the little huff of breath she released. "Look, I'll show you."

She took his journal from her lap and flipped it open. It was one of his earlier journals, mostly showing sketches of the internal structures of animals. There was a time in his life when he would take the opportunity to dissect any animal he found dead for the sake of discovering its inner secrets. The practice had lost much of its appeal with age as he began to see the evidence of suffering inside bodies. It hardly seemed like appropriate reading material for the moment, these sketches of organs and bones. But Maëlle held up the page that showed a carefully cut open earthworm, the internal organs each neatly labeled in Talos's metered handwriting.

"Earthworms have five hearts. Five! Would you argue that they love?"

Talos frowned. "No. But their hearts are not as complicated as a human heart."

Maëlle made a noise of frustration and flipped to a new page. This time she showed a bear, with a close view of the thoracic cavity. The heart was at the center, the flesh-and-blood engine that ran the whole. "Bear hearts look almost exactly the same as human ones. Do bears love?"

Talos remembered the bear vividly. It had been one of the specimens that led him away from dissections. She had been protecting her cubs from a larger male bear, one who had won the fight. He felt a shiver of disquiet at the memory. Maëlle couldn't know that history—he hadn't preserved it in his notes—but it still hung in the air between them like a net too fine to see.

"Maybe," he said. "They will protect their cubs, even at the expense of their own life. They care for them. Maybe they love them, too."

"They care for them—the way you care for your brother? Like Raffa cares for you, too?"

"I..." Talos felt like he was chasing Maëlle through a forest, barely catching glimpses of her thoughts as she ran. "It's not the same as love. There's no romance. No...carnal desires."

"Love and sex are not synonyms, Talos. Carnal desire isn't required for love. All love means is that there's someone you're passionate about, someone you care for and want to protect and see happy. Someone you want to spend time with. Someone you feel belongs with you, who fits with you, who feels right next to you."

Something about Maëlle's words made Talos uncomfortable. He felt an imaginary fault line down his middle, slowly grinding stone on stone, grating and on the edge of pain. She couldn't be right, could she? Love couldn't be something so simple and straightforward as that? It was a complicated human thing, a matter of heart and lust and marriage, not just someone who feels right next to you.

"Carnal love is only one kind of love," she continued. "You can have platonic love for a friend, someone who you're very close to but feel no romantic attachment to. You can love things or experiences, like strawberries or flying. You can love family—that's the love you and Raffa have for each other, whether you believe it or not. And the love between a mother bear and her cubs. Care for each other, caring about each other."

Her eyes, which had been so serious and intent up until this moment, went suddenly soft and wide and a little wet, like rain puddles reflecting blue sky. "And there's romantic love, too, which doesn't have to be associated with carnal love. Two people can be romantically in love without being..." She paused, the blush lighting her cheeks. "Without being sexually involved."

"But then how do you have children?"

Talos hadn't meant to ask the question, hadn't even known it was bubbling to the front of his mind, but the idea of humans experiencing romantic love without the biological need to reproduce seemed to contradict everything he knew about nature. In all of his observations of the natural world, in every animal he ever watched, the ultimate goal was always children.

He could tell as soon as the words were in the air between them that it was the wrong thing to ask. Maëlle's expression closed down in an instant. It was like a cloud passing over the sun. Something dark moved behind her eyes, something big and sad and hurtful. She dropped her gaze to her hands, clutched together at her waist, fingers knotted together like pieces of a puzzle box.

"Children are not always part of love," she said, and her voice was the whisper of a moth's wings against flame. Her grip tightened, her knuckles whitening against themselves. "Not part of every person's life. I'm...broken inside. Barren." She said the word like a curse. "I'll never have children."

Talos didn't understand why it made her so sad. He didn't understand a lot and lacked the physiology of flesh to draw on for empathy. But he did know that he wanted to brush the pain from her face, to untangle her knotted fingers one by one with gentle kisses.

And at the same time, he also felt lost and adrift, everything about Maëlle's words clashing with Raffa's, confusing and contrary and...unnatural? Was that right? Or was it completely natural? He didn't know how to feel, what to do. He was buzzing inside, friction and chaos and transmutation. It was like something taking root, or something metamorphosizing, or something exploding. He clutched a hand to his chest, trying to still the feeling and keep himself from vibrating apart.

"Maëlle," he said, feeling something that could be pain in his chest under his grasping hand. The pink of sunrise was fading from her skin, and he yearned to catch the last traces of it on his fingertips. "Why are you telling me this?"

She wrapped her arms around her knees again, folding in on herself like she could become small enough to disappear. Her eyes wavered with tears, the blue of them shatteringly clear and depthless. "Because I want you to know you can be happy, Talos. That love is open to you. I want you to understand it. I want you to *believe* it. Even if...even if it's not with me."

Not with Maëlle.

Happy without Maëlle?

The words went through him like a chisel, like a spear, like a bolt of lightning. He felt too full of words and thoughts and ideas and—and emotions. How did humans manage this chaos? He clutched his head as if he could hold himself together physically, trying to will some semblance of order into his thoughts. But they buzzed and swelled and swirled; they vibrated inside him until he swore he was going to shake apart into a million grains of sand at Maëlle's feet. He needed...he needed time to think. He needed space. He needed...

Maëlle reached a gentle hand towards him, ready to take his arm or smooth his brow, clearly concerned. If she touched him now, he might not ever regain coherence. He pulled back, afraid of himself.

"I have to go," he said, rising abruptly.

He held his head still and squeezed his eyes shut against Maëlle's half-teary look. He couldn't stand to look at her, not now. He might explode in her face if he did, propelled to a million pieces by everything boiling up inside. So instead, he ran and left her by the strawberries in the new day's light.

Chapter Eleven

Maëlle watched Talos go at a near run, disappearing down steeper rocks than she could follow, wings flared wide for the sake of balance on the treacherous terrain. And her heart went with him, a shattered thing she had tied to the curve of his smile. It left her hollow and numb.

Such a fool. She had thought that if she explained things, if she used examples and language Talos would be familiar with, he might understand. She had thought she could tell him how she felt. But then he had brought up children, and she had remembered how broken she was. An empty, worthless thing. How could she admit to loving him in the shadow of that revelation? And when he was the one specifically to ask about children in the first place? So she had balked, and now he was gone. He was gone, and she was cold and bare and raw, the void of being alone the only thing inside.

She needed some air. She needed some perspective. She needed to *fly*.

She rode Arwa for hours, clutching her like the gryphon's feathers and fur and warmth were the only thing keeping her alive. Arwa had endurance to spare. She was happy to catch the mountain updrafts and swoop over peaks and cliffs, even when the winds picked up and the clouds moved in. Maëlle felt sure it would rain soon, but she couldn't bring herself to care enough to land. Where would she go, anyway? Back to Talos's home, where his angry brother Raffa waited? Was Talos even home again yet? Arwa circled in ever-widening loops around Talos's home, the center of a bullseye that Maëlle was moving farther and farther away from.

Movement caught Maëlle's eye. There was a flicker of hope inside the void of her heart, a tiny yearning that she would see Talos. Instead, she saw the horses and the finery and the flag bearing the familiar family crest and was suddenly crushed by reality returning. Even before she brought Arwa lower, she recognized Gaubert's form. He raised a hand towards her—not in greeting but as if he could pluck her from the sky. A gesture of ownership.

She should land and speak with him, she knew. She should go back with him; the marriage was set for the day after tomorrow, and the fact that he was here in the mountains must mean he intended to continue with those wedding plans. But she'd had too many days of freedom and wanted another moment of selfishness.

Or, rather, what she wanted was one more chance to speak with Talos. To explain. Or, at least, to say goodbye.

She tilted Arwa's wings back and forth once, acknowledging Gaubert's presence, then flew back up the mountain towards Talos's home. Behind her, though she heard nothing, she could see Gaubert waving his arms and yelling in anger. He would not appreciate her decision. She would need to accept that when she saw him next.

She brought Arwa down by the strawberry garden and slid from her back. She wanted to find Talos here, among his plants, paying them the careful attention he always did. But she circled the garden and saw no sign of him. The blustery wind tossed her hair into her face, shaking the grass thatch sunshade until she was afraid it would come to pieces. There were no bees out in this weather, and even most of the flowers had closed at the chill in the air.

She paused long enough to find one red strawberry among the leaves, holding it in her hand to warm it like that could mimic the experience of a sun-warmed strawberry on her tongue.

Instead, the sweetness tasted dull and cloying, the seeds gritty in her teeth. The pulp sat heavy and acidic in her stomach.

The first drops of rain pattered against her as she climbed down the narrow rock path to the patio below. Somewhere distant, the faint growl of faraway thunder cleared its throat. She looked to the western horizon, seeing the black clouds hanging low there beyond the dull gray ones already in the sky. The wind was blowing mostly north, so it would be slow in coming, but when the storm hit, it would be bad.

"I thought you left."

The voice wasn't soft, and it wasn't kind, and it wasn't familiar. It wasn't Talos. She turned to see another lithander on the patio, arms crossed across his broad granite chest. He was bigger than Talos and sharper, too. He had the ears and toothy muzzle of a wolf but the size and posture of a bear, and claws on his knuckles that were each as long as her hand.

"You're Talos's brother."

"Raffa En-Klint." Talos's older brother, then. En meant first child if her books were to be believed. "And you're Talos's pet human."

She winced, wondering if it was true. Had she just been a curiosity to him? Something to study, like he studied bees and flowers and rocks? She had thought it was more, that there had been something real building between them. But the way Talos had acted when she spoke to him of love—he had run away. She wasn't sure she understood anything about him anymore.

"Is Talos home again yet?" she asked.

Raffa shifted his stance, subtly putting himself more firmly between her and the doorway. "I'm here on his behalf. Talos needs you to leave. Now."

The words were a knife to her chest, slicing her already raw heart deeper and rougher. She swallowed past the pain. "Don't worry. I'm leaving. I just...wanted to say goodbye first."

"No."

Almost two weeks staying with Talos, and he wouldn't even let her in to say goodbye? He couldn't even face her? He had to rely on his brother as gatekeeper? She looked past Raffa's hulking form at the yawning doorway and wondered if Talos was there, watching her from the darkness inside, unable to face her. Far off, thunder moved. Fat drops of rain stitched the stone patio in the intermittent staccato of an impending storm.

"Talos!" she yelled, watching for some sign of movement in the dark—some flinch or shifting or withdrawing. She saw nothing except Raffa's granite form stepping closer to her. He had his teeth bared, hands fisted so tightly at his sides, the long claws quivered.

"I won't let you hurt him," Raffa said. "Go, little human, before I start feeling less generous."

The pain was cold and sharp, something that might eat Maëlle from the inside out. But she wouldn't beg—not even for the sake of Talos and his gentle nature. "Tell him thank you, then," she said, drawing her cloak tighter around her. "For everything."

Raffa let out a low growl, and for a moment, she thought it was for her—angry that she had the audacity to thank Talos or maybe just angry that she treated Raffa as a messenger. But he was looking beyond her, down the gravel path, and his dark flint eyes were intense. Maëlle turned to look too, and saw horses and riders approaching. Gaubert, she realized. He and his men must have followed her. Their horses were breathing hard, lather starkly pale against their dark coats; clearly, they had been pushed hard, maybe even past their limit.

"More humans," he snarled. "You brought them here, didn't you?" He took a step towards Maëlle, menace in every angle of his stone frame.

"Stay," she said, holding up a hand to him. Remarkably, it worked. "I'm leaving with them. We won't bother you."

Raffa narrowed his eyes at the oncoming party, clearly seeing the family crest on the flag as it fluttered in the high winds. "Desroches." He spat the name like something bitter and old.

"My fiancé," Maëlle admitted, letting out a breath that felt like her last. She turned from Raffa, turned from Talos, turned from the home in the mountain and the strawberry patch and the comfortable memories of belonging, and walked to where Gaubert approached.

"Is that a lithander?" Gaubert asked, incredulous. "Have you been hiding with one of the stone men?"

"Leave him alone, Gaubert."

"Savage beasts." He had a scowl on his face that looked ready to grind stone, and Maëlle remembered that his grandfather had lost a leg in the last war with the lithander.

"He's not important," she insisted, then whistled for Arwa.

Gaubert shook his head, refocusing his attention on her instead. He made an attempt to school the anger from his face. It surprised Maëlle that he would put forth even that minimal effort on her behalf. "I've been searching for you for days. Will you come home, Maëlle? The wedding is the day after tomorrow."

She had a duty to this man and to her father. Engagement was a contract of sorts. She didn't love Gaubert and never would, and he scared her still. But she would learn how to manage his anger. She would learn when to speak and when to remain quiet, how to approach him, when to leave the house. She couldn't give him children, but he couldn't give her happiness. It seemed a marriage doomed to mutual dissatisfaction, balanced and contracted. Human customs had never felt quite so alien to her before.

Arwa landed and pushed her heart-shaped face under Maëlle's arm. Maëlle scratched the gryphon's neck, and the touch of warm feathers and cold rain drops mingled on her skin, echoing the definition of bittersweet. She looked back once more. Raffa still stood guard, claws out like a protector statue. The wind didn't move him, though it blew leaves and grass around the patio in a miniature a tornado, churning up the debris of life. There was no sign of Talos at all.

"Yes," she said to Gaubert, tearing her eyes away from the home in the mountainside. "Let's go."

After all, she had nowhere else to be.

Chapter Twelve

Talos felt the impending storm through the rock of the mountain well before he saw the black clouds on the distant horizon. At first, he mistook the rumbling for the continued turmoil in his mind. There could well be a thunderstorm inside him for all the chaos.

He climbed mountains with a single-minded focus, looking to wear himself out or distract himself from his thoughts or find clarity amongst all the buzzing. He felt swarmed by information and ideas, revelations, Maëlle's words and explanations, emotions. He wanted to stop climbing long enough to hold himself together so he didn't come apart with everything in his head. But stopping was worse. Stopping would let his thoughts catch up with him. So he kept climbing.

Down, up, over, through. He knew these mountains like he knew the rock of his own hand. He could climb without thinking, each foot and handhold expected and secure. Eventually, the pattern of it started to calm him. It let him order his thoughts, sort and process them, file them away appropriately. He reached the peak of one of the taller mounts, and the wind buffeted him with unexpected fury. It wouldn't knock him free—he weighed too much for that—but it brushed past him with an abrasive force he hadn't expected. The day's light had turned dull and gray. Far in the distance to the west, he saw a line of clouds as black as soot. He felt the thunder through the mountain again. He should not be here—should not be so high in the mountains with a thunderstorm on the horizon. Lightning was dangerous for the lithander—one of the few things that was.

Maybe love was another.

He sat on a stone outcrop on a cliff that was otherwise nearly vertical and watched the clouds boil to the west. Talos couldn't remember ever reaching such a state of confusion before. It had panicked him. Now, with his thoughts swarming less, he could see more clearly. He could understand everything Maëlle had been saying and could realize the truth of it. Climbing had always been a way for Talos to clear his mind, and it had worked this time too. Except for the one thing he couldn't get out of his head, no matter how much he scrabbled up mountains.

Hours later, Maëlle was still there, clear as crystal. Maybe she lived inside him now. He didn't dislike the idea. And no matter what Maëlle had said, what she thought, he had realized something during his climbing: he wouldn't be happy without her.

Was that love? The romantic kind of love? Maëlle had insisted love was about passion and care, protection and happiness, comfort and belonging. Someone who feels right next to you. Talos felt all of that for Maëlle, the delicate human who was stronger than expected, who pushed back against the stone, the one with honey hair and glacial lake eyes and a voice like shivering crystal. She did feel right next to him. Even now, it felt wrong to know she wasn't there.

Love, he mused. Was it really? Why had no lithander untangled this truth before? Maybe it was the constant warring between lithander and humans. Maybe a need to feel different or stronger than their human rivals. Maybe it was just a misunderstanding of physiology and psychology. Whatever the reason, the more Talos thought about it, the more convinced he was that he understood love. That he felt love. That he loved Maëlle.

And he had left her alone in the strawberry garden, with only Raffa there for company.

Talos had to get back, he realized, as the first fat drops of rain spattered lazily on his stone wings. He didn't think Raffa would hurt Maëlle—not when he knew she was important to Talos. But it would certainly be tense and uncomfortable.

Besides, he felt cold without Maëlle near him. He wanted that heat back, the one that lit him up inside like magma.

It was raining in earnest by the time he got home, sheets of water sluicing from his stone body as he climbed. He had heard thunder approaching, like a lumbering beast—unwieldy and slow but growing closer. The wind ran through the mountain as strong and skittish as stampeding elk. He paused just long enough to take down the wind-broken sunshade over the strawberry patch, and the first lightning cracked the sky as he was climbing down from the garden.

He dropped the remains of the soggy grass sunshade just inside the door, shaking water from his surface to keep from tracking it inside. The fire was built up, giving the stone room real warmth in addition to a cozy sort of warm light.

"Maëlle?" he asked, looking by the fire. He expected to find her curled up by the light, reading one of his journals, maybe. Instead, the chairs near the fire had been pushed back, and a large block of granite stood in the full light, Raffa making marks on the surface with a stick of ragged charcoal.

"She's gone," Raffa said, not looking up from his careful measurements and studying.

Talos stopped cold, grabbing the doorway for support. It felt like the mountainside was tipping under him, and he would slide right off the edge if not careful. "What?"

"Left with that fiancé of hers."

She...left? After their conversation? After talk of love and romance and belonging? And with Gaubert, of all people?

"No," he said. He wanted to convince himself as much as Raffa, like he could make it not true if he just believed hard enough. "She wouldn't go with him."

"Humans want human company," Raffa said. "I told you as much."

Talos could swear he felt a fault line open up right through his middle, cracking with enough force to split continents. The heat inside him all drained free, lava spilling from a crevice. It left him feeling as hollow and brittle as an eggshell. One tap, and he might break in on himself. He couldn't seem to hold himself up and found he had slid to the floor with a soft thump.

Raffa looked at him finally, clearly surprised to find Talos on the floor. There must have been something on Talos's face or in his eyes that made Raffa worry. Maybe he could tell how empty Talos felt or see the cracks running through him. Whatever the case, he put down his stick of charcoal with a frown and came to stand by Talos.

"She's not good for you, brother," he said, offering Talos a hand up. "And you're not good for her either. It's better this way."

"Better," Talos said, and he almost choked on the mirthless laugh. He didn't need to breathe and still felt like he couldn't get enough air. "She's not safe, not with Gaubert. How is that better?"

Raffa's expression hardened, flint eyes going darker as he took his hand back. "Gaubert—the Desroches boy? No surprises there."

Talos snapped his gaze to Raffa's like a magnet to iron. "You know him?"

"I know the family. It was a Desroches that maimed Sándor—did you know that? I fought many of them in the last war. Killed a couple of them myself. Every last one was violent and mean."

"Then you know," Talos accused. He felt a new fire in him, but this one was different. It was angry and fierce, and it roared in his empty chest as hot and hungry as a wildfire looking to devour the entire mountainside. He rose, pushing back to his feet as the thunder boomed outside. "He will be violent and mean to Maëlle too. He has already."

"She must be the same to willingly take his name," Raffa said, stubborn as stone.

"No." Talos snapped the word like ice fracturing. "She's different—I told you that. She's kind and gentle, and he will break her. Like they broke Sándor."

For the first time, Raffa looked unsure. Their absent middle sibling was a sore subject for them both, and Talos almost felt bad wielding Raffa's guilt as a weapon now. But Talos shook his head. He had no time for his brother's closed-minded attitude. He...he needed to go get Maëlle. He needed to save her from Gaubert. He needed her to know that he loved her.

"Did she say anything before going?" he asked, storming around the room to collect his bag and what supplies he thought he might need. "Anything that might tell me where the Desroches manor house might be?"

Raffa seemed pensive, shifting from foot to foot. "All she said was to thank you."

Talos swore, pulling down journals from his stacks until he found the one he was looking for. He had done some mapping during his wandering, but his sketches and maps focused almost entirely on the mountains and not the lowlands nearby where the humans lived. He flipped page after page, looking for some clue as to where there might be large manor houses near the mountains—some clue as to where Gaubert had taken Maëlle. Why had he ignored human settlements in his maps? It had been short-sighted, and now, it might mean the difference between finding Maëlle and—

Raffa caught his arm, and Talos glared at him with the full force of the anger burning inside him. "I have to do this, Raffa."

For a moment, Raffa said nothing. He seemed to be warring with himself, maybe fighting against his better judgment. But eventually, he let Talos go, and Talos saw the change in him. His brother had never been a flexible person, and it was difficult for him to alter his opinions. But he made an effort now, no doubt for Talos's sake. Talos saw it and knew it as evidence of love—the kind of familial love Maëlle had described. He wanted to hug his brother for it even as he wanted to punch him.

"I know where Desroches Manor is," Raffa said like the words were being pulled from him by horses.

Talos let out a noise halfway between sob and hope. He flipped his journal around, handing it to Raffa. "Where?"

Raffa glanced at the pages, then shook his head. He grumbled something, as low and heavy as a crashing avalanche. "Come, brother. I'll show you."

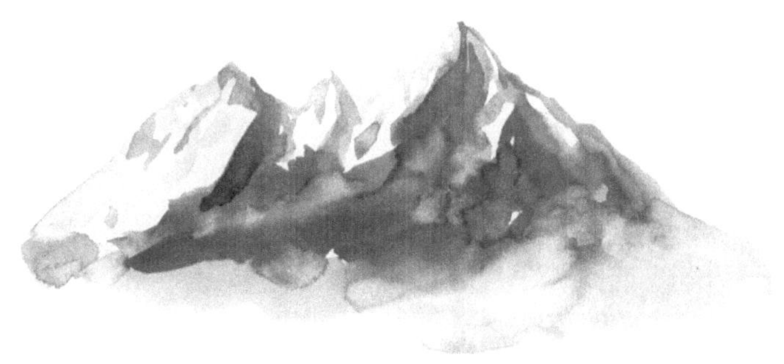

Chapter Thirteen

I t felt strange to have so many people around again. Maëlle had grown to love the quiet and solitude of living with Talos, but now, back at Gaubert's manor, there were dozens of people around all the time. Half a dozen lady's maids helped her remove her stained and soaked riding clothes, helped her bathe, helped brush her hair, and put her in an evening dress. They chattered constantly, like a flock of chickadees—pretty voices, but Maëlle had trouble paying attention to the words. She wished instead for the crackle of fire and the sound of pencil on paper, the expressive silences and small noises of companionship, gentle conversation to fill the corners of the hours, the chance for her to sing for someone who wanted to hear her voice.

Dinner felt bloated and overwrought. She hadn't eaten meat in almost two weeks, and the sight of a rare cut of venison made her stomach roil. She ate the bread and the roasted root vegetables, picking listlessly at the pale chicken flesh on her plate.

Gaubert was carefully genteel over dinner. She could tell it wasn't an attempt at changing his behavior—merely a way to placate her until the wedding. He asked Maëlle meaningless but polite questions. What jewels she would wear to the wedding. What kind of flowers should be on their table. Whether she preferred fish or veal for the reception dinner. She almost said she wanted neither and demanded big baskets of strawberries instead, with sprays of mountain lupines and peasant cornflowers on the tables. But Gaubert never asked about Talos or Raffa, and so she returned the courtesy by not trying to agitate him in front of his family.

Several of Gaubert's relatives had arrived for the wedding already, and the table was packed with aunts, uncles, and cousins. They got louder the more they drank. A pair of Gaubert's younger female cousins asked Maëlle how her sun-pinked and wind-chapped skin had gotten so uncomfortably ruddy. An older uncle implied loudly and in her general direction that it was unladylike to ride gryphons—or maybe to ride any animal at all. A gaggle of cousins who were of an age with Gaubert clustered near the groom and snickered behind their hands, heads bowed close to one another in conspiracy.

Maëlle didn't care much about their jibes, but even before the dessert course, she was feeling claustrophobic and overstimulated. There were too many people, too much noise. Belligerent loudness. She escaped to the library the first chance she had. It had always been the one room in the house where she felt comfortable—quiet, orderly, full of books, and with a conspicuous lack of Gaubert. But even there, she found maids dusting and cleaning the floors, shaking the drapes, and cleaning the ashes from the fireplace. People were everywhere in this house, and she had never noticed the sheer number of them before.

She browsed the titles until she felt the weight of too many eyes watching her. Then she took a stack of books, ignoring the annoyed look of the butler straightening the shelves, and headed for her rooms instead. She was just wondering whether Gaubert's Aunt Pruen would still be asleep in the chair by the fire, just as she had been when Maëlle left for dinner, when she overheard Gaubert's loud voice from the nearby study clearly speaking her father's name.

She paused, hearing the round of half-drunk laughter from Gaubert's male cousins. The smell of whiskey and cigars leaked through the slightly ajar door.

"So ship the wench back," one of the cousins slurred. "She can't give you an heir, right? You were sold defective goods."

Maëlle winced, tasting an iron-rich bile at the back of her throat. Was Gaubert really insensitive enough to complain about her inability to have children with people she had never even met before? She supposed the question of an heir made it a family matter, but it still made her feel ill hearing those unknown male voices talk about her faulty womb like they had some claim of ownership over it.

Gaubert made a noise that was half-growl, and she heard the sound of a bottle being uncorked, liquid sloshing into a cup. "Elouan Le Gwenneg won't commit the bride price until his worthless daughter is safely married, the good-for-nothing boor. The Le Gwennegs have none of the qualities of the upper class except for money, so he's lucky he has a lot of it."

"Then how will you produce an heir?" another cousin asked.

"There's always the chamber maids," a third cousin offered, once again to roars of laughter.

It didn't surprise Maëlle that Gaubert's cousins were as uncouth as he was. Their words made her cringe, even though the idea that Gaubert might seek another woman's bed was something of a relief. Beyond consummation of the marriage, what reason would he have to force himself on her? But she didn't really want to hear more of the men's rowdy, bawdy conversation. She was just turning to go again when Gaubert replied, and it was the cold, steely tone of his voice that made her stop in her tracks.

"I will not have a bastard heir."

The words cut through her like a sheet of ice, freezing her to the spine. She felt for a moment like she couldn't breathe from the chill of it, like her boots had been iced to the floor, like her eyes were fogged with the traceries of frost. The hardness in his words was absolute. How was it that this flesh-and-blood mortal could be so much harder than a lithander made of literal stone?

"Divorce?" one of the cousins suggested.

"Le Gwenneg accounted for that possibility in the bride contract," Gaubert said, voice bitter. "But...accidents do happen. Nothing can stop a widower from remarrying."

Maëlle exhaled as sharply as if she had been punched. The chill that had frozen her in place evaporated suddenly, like steam in the face of her flaring anger's heat. This man would sit here, barely a day before their wedding, and plot her death for the sake of money and legitimate heirs? Gaubert was a monster. She had thought—had convinced herself—that he wouldn't hurt her again, that she could learn how to manage his temper, that the bride price was worth too much to the Desroches coffers. She had let herself think that her duty to her father and contracts made in her name were more important than being happy. But Gaubert would not only hurt her again; he would hurt her more. Would even kill her.

She should have known better. Should have guessed she couldn't stay. Should have learned by now.

And maybe Gaubert should have learned by now, too, she thought, storming down the hall toward her rooms. She had escaped last time because he was too busy getting drunk to pay her attention and maybe because he thought she wouldn't be fool enough to go out in the rain. And here she was, only six hours home, and he was drunk again, and it was raining again, and she was leaving again—and still no one tried to stop her.

She planned better this time, packing a couple changes of clothes, a purse of coins, and a few pieces of jewelry that had belonged to her mother. She wrapped a couple of her favorite books in layers of waxed linen, packing them tightly in a water-proof bag. She found her wool cloak to wear against the wet. She took some carrots and apples from the kitchen, too, though she knew she could feed herself now by foraging, thanks to Talos's training.

A twinge ate at the core of her anger, thinking the lithander's name, but she put it to the side for now. He hadn't wanted her. Had pulled back from her touch. Had sent Raffa to get rid of her. That was clearly over. She would find a place alone in the woods where she and Arwa could have a cottage. Maybe in the forested foothills of the mountains. She winced, realizing that would put her halfway between Gaubert and Talos. No—maybe she would fly past the mountains, over them, and to the other side instead. There must be forests there, too, surely.

The storm was still venting its fury outside, thunder and lightning punching the air. The wind drove the rain into biting needles. Even the covered walkway to the stables was wet, and Maëlle was soaked to her knees before she even reached Arwa.

"Shh," she whispered, stroking Arwa's face feathers. She sent the stableboy away, finding the gryphon saddle and tightening it around Arwa herself. "Don't worry, lovely. I won't make you fly in this. We'll head for the woods until the weather calms." Arwa groomed her beak through Maëlle's hair, huffing air along her neck. "Troublemaker! You know that tickles. Come on."

The rain almost blinded her, but she knew the direction, and Arwa stuck her head under Maëlle's arm to help keep her steady. The protection of the Desroches family woods lessened the assault, but only marginally. The trees above were whipping to and fro in the wind, as flexible as giant sheaves of wheat. Lightning struck in the mountains, somewhere close enough that the crack of its thunder almost knocked Maëlle from her feet.

Maybe she should have waited for the storm to cease or at least for the lightning to stop. But as soon as she knew Gaubert's true plans, she hadn't been able to stay. It was too much—the pain and fear, the perilous situation ready to break. Anything would be better than living in that shadow, even for one more night.

Another bolt of lightning streaked overhead, lighting the sky for an instant. Arwa's pelt rippled in distress at the crash of thunder. The gryphon had her heart-shaped face tucked solidly against Maëlle's side now, trying to hide from the storm.

"Come on," she said, leading Arwa onward. "There are some caves by the river on the other side of the woods. We can shelter there, my lovely."

Ahead, a tree cracked in half under the wind, the top falling to the ground in a crashing avalanche of wood and leaf. Arwa jumped, head tossing to look at the fallen tree. A moment later, she bolted.

"Arwa! No, wait!"

Maëlle raced after her, but the gryphon was fast, even when wings weren't involved. The wet ground slid beneath Maëlle's boots, leaves and needles falling from the trees to be whipped by the lash of the relentless wind. In the dark and the rain, it became harder and harder to track Arwa's racing shape, despite her white fur.

"Arwa!" she called again, desperate not to lose her only friend because she had been too impatient to wait out a storm.

The gryphon stopped short, wings flared until the feathers whistled in the wind. A male voice cried out in alarm. And Maëlle's heart forgot how to beat.

That voice...

Lightning briefly lit her way, and she ran to Arwa's side. The gryphon was standing over something that moved on the ground, one paw holding it down. But she wasn't making noises of alarm, and her feathers and fur weren't ruffled. Instead, she purred in recognition and affectionately rubbed her face against the form.

"Arwa?" the male voice asked, and Maëlle knew it was him, even before the next flash of lightning showed her granite, stone wings, and a pretty carved face. Talos. "Where is—" he started to ask the gryphon, but Maëlle's knees went weak, and she had to wrap her arms around Arwa's neck to keep upright. She wasn't ready to see him again—maybe she never would be. It broke something inside her when his jasper red eyes found her in the dark, caught on her like a cloak snagged on thorns, recognized her with resounding certainty. "Maëlle," he said, and it was benediction and knife at once.

"Why are you here?" she asked, her voice croaking. A flash of purple lightning streaked the sky, and she rubbed her cheek further into Arwa's neck feathers. "It's not safe. The lightning."

Talos sat up, glancing at the sky only once. "Lightning is as dangerous for you as it is for me," he pointed out. A low rumble of thunder vibrated Maëlle's bones.

"I didn't have to come through the mountains."

For a moment, Talos just studied her as if he could read her entire history in the fall of wet hair in her eyes. "I had to come."

"Why are you here, Talos?" she asked again and felt her voice breaking on his name like a physical tear at the back of her throat.

She swallowed past the pain, stepping Arwa back to let the lithander get to his feet. He flexed his stone wings, then flared them wide, curving one up over Maëlle's head like an umbrella.

It only stopped half the rain but made her feel closer to him. Intimate in a way that ached deep in her chest.

"I came to...save you. From Gaubert," he said. "He's not a good person—Raffa told me about his family." Talos looked through the dark trees, as if he might see Raffa or Gaubert there. "He fought the Desroches in the war. I don't want Gaubert to hurt you again. So...we came."

His words petered out at the end like he wasn't sure how to finish. He was hesitant and unsure in that endearing way of his. Part of her wanted to go to him, to wrap arms around him and reassure him that she was ok, but at the mention of Raffa's name, she saw the larger lithander in her memory, teeth bared, arms crossed, blocking the way to Talos. The impassible gate Talos had set in front of her.

"I can take care of myself," she said, and it was half snap and half sob, the words loud in the sudden lull of a break between wind gusts. She saw the words hit Talos, the flinch, the tiny pinch of eyes, the twitch of wings. It hurt her to hurt him, too, but maybe it was needed. Cut the bonds cleanly.

Talos rubbed the back of his neck, rain sluicing over his shoulders, clearly seeing her packed bags hanging from Arwa's saddle. "I guess that's true," he said. He took a moment to form the next words, as if testing and discarding several options. He looked so fragile for a thing made of stone, like he was collapsing in on himself in the weather. "Where will you go?"

It was an impersonal question, a polite inquiry, and that ripped Maëlle up inside more than anything else so far. She had to turn away, afraid he might see tears in her eyes despite the masking rain, and busied herself with checking Arwa's saddle and bags.

"Away." She said it as firmly as she could manage and not nearly as firmly as she would have preferred.

Talos stood by silently while Maëlle checked every single strap and binding, doing nothing more than shifting his wing slightly to keep her covered as she worked. Arwa stood between them, heart-shaped face looking back and forth, cocking curiously to one side and then the other.

There was lightning still in the sky. Maëlle considered whether she should make Talos come to the nearby river caves with her, to get out of the storm—out of harm's way. Part of her, a vindictive little seed buried deep, wanted to send him away; if he had been fool enough to come out in this storm, he deserved to be fool enough to wander home in it. But she couldn't do it, not even now when he held the shattered pieces of her heart between his stone fingers like some pretty insect to study and sketch. How could she wish any harm to this gentle man? He was as soft as morning fog, and she would gladly bruise herself on the stone of him if it would mean anything to him.

"I'm sorry I wasn't home when Gaubert came," Talos said quietly, the drumming of rain almost enough to wash the words away.

And yet, for all their gentleness, his words grabbed her heart and squeezed. She spun to face him. He looked miserable in the rain, though the wet shouldn't bother him. Rainwater collected in the curves of his stone eyelashes until it looked like he was crying. He wasn't there at home? But...if Talos hadn't been home, why had Raffa—

"Halt!"

The cry cut Maëlle's thoughts short. She recognized the voice, slightly slurry with alcohol as it was, and it was the last person she wanted to see right now. To see ever. But when she turned, he was there anyway: Gaubert, in an expensive waterproof cloak, with a sword on his hip and a gaggle of brawny cousins arrayed behind him.

"Gaubert," she said, the fear and exasperation warring inside her.

Before she could say more, Talos was stepping in front of her, wings folded behind him again, acting as a shield against her fiancé's anger. But there was no malice in his movements, no threat. The way he moved clearly said that the idea of violence would only ever be one-sided, and he was impervious to it. Having seen Raffa, Maëlle knew that wasn't true. Stone could hit hard if needed. But she couldn't imagine Talos swinging fists or weapons, not even to protect something important to him.

She, on the other hand, would gladly punch Gaubert right in his arrogant, sneering face if she knew anything about punching.

"You have something that belongs to me, grotesque." Gaubert's cousins sniggered cruelly at the rude slur, and Maëlle bristled.

"No. Maëlle belongs only to herself," Talos said, voice calm. And sweet lord, if she wasn't already hopelessly in love with this man, that would have been enough to steal her heart.

"Go away, Gaubert," she said, stepping up to stand beside Talos. Thunder rumbled the ground, and she felt it echo through her chest. "I'm not going back with you."

He pointed an angry finger at Maëlle. "Harlot! Your father sold you to me, fair and square. We have a contract!"

"Your contract can rot in a shallow grave, you monster. Did you really think I would marry you just so you could kill me the next day?"

For a second, Gaubert's eyes went wild. He clearly hadn't expected Maëlle to figure out his plan or to call him on it. But that chaos quickly solidified into real rage, and he marched in her direction, fists clenched. On one side of her, Talos went supernaturally still. On her other side, Arwa crouched and hissed, feathers fluffed and fur on end. "You worthless, broken—"

Talos put out an arm and stopped Gaubert before he could reach Maëlle. He didn't shove or hit Gaubert—just provided a barrier. A stone gate, stronger than the flesh Gaubert was made of so that he bounced off it like he had hit a wall. But Gaubert was so furious he couldn't think straight, clearly. He turned on Talos, the anger boiling off him as violent as thunder.

And he stepped forward, swinging a punch at Talos.

Maëlle saw the moment of surprise on Talos's face, knew the moment he realized what would happen. He only had time to shift half a step backward before Gaubert's fist hit him solidly on the chin. A crack rang through the woods, like the sound of a tree branch snapping.

And then Gaubert was howling in pain, clutching his broken hand to his chest.

Maëlle wondered how many bones he had broken in his hand. It was his own fault, thinking he could punch pure granite. Even Talos's attempt to soften the blow couldn't soften it enough to spare him. Gaubert had always been a hothead, an idiot, and an ass. She wouldn't regret it if she never saw him again.

"Vile creature," Gaubert hissed through his teeth, the words tinged with the whimper of pain. With his unbroken left hand, he awkwardly drew his sword. Around him, a dozen of his scowling cousins drew weapons of their own. "I will not let some heartless stone beast take what's mine!"

Talos once again put himself between Maëlle and Gaubert, and Arwa leaned forward in a threat of her own. But it was movement in the forest to the side that snagged Maëlle's attention. Through darkness and close tree trunks, something approached—a nightmare of stone and claw, as unstoppable as a rockslide. Her breath caught, and she gripped Talos's arm to keep from running. A roar, louder than the howling wind and nearly as deafening as the thunder, shuddered through the air. Then a mountain of granite reared up in front of the Desroches men.

"You dare strike my brother?" Raffa roared.

Gaubert staggered a step backward, leaning heavily on his sword for support, and who could blame him? Raffa towered over him, eight feet tall and built more of rage than stone. Cowed, hand broken, sloppy with drink and fear, Gaubert had melted from a man of power to a pitiable and breakable thing.

"We're leaving now," Maëlle said. "Don't follow me. I won't come back."

Alcohol or ego or the need to prove himself in front of his cousins gave Gaubert a fleeting sense of false bravado, just enough to artificially stiffen his spine. "Two lithander?" he scoffed. "Even if you've been whoring yourself out to two grotesques, Maëlle, you're still mine. You're not going any-where."

As Gaubert spat the last words, he lunged. His sword re-mained point-down in the wet loam. Instead, he reached into his coat and pulled free a short-handled throwing axe. With a practiced flick of his wrist, he sent the weapon flying end over end in Maëlle's direction, the metal flashing blue with reflected lightning, the edge slicing through the heavy rain.

Time seemed to drip as slow as cold resin, the seconds between lightning flashes stretching into long minutes. Arwa reared back, hissing and growling, front paws held high and claws out. Maëlle raised her arms to ward off the axe, worried for Arwa. And Talos stepped in front of her and Arwa both, flaring his stone wings wide as a shield.

The axe made contact, the sound bright and sharp and painful, metal on stone. It rebounded from Talos's wing to land heavily in the mud. Half a second later, a chip of granite no larger than Maëlle's thumb and shaped like a fine feather splashed into the puddle near the downed weapon.

Talos didn't flinch or cry out in pain, but Maëlle did on his behalf.

"Talos! Your wing!"

But before she could inspect the injury, Raffa roared once more, and this time the thunder crashed simultaneously, amplifying and echoing his rage. The rain picked up in intensity, as if feeding from Raffa's anger. Lightning flashed, blindingly, close enough to nearly knock Maëlle off her feet. In stormy silhouette, Raffa raised his hands into fists, the blades there showing sharp and strong as a threat. He could be a god made of the mountain itself, the storm incarnate, unleashed fury.

"I have blades, too, Desroches," Raffa growled. "And you've given me ample reason to use them."

It was too much; how could it not be? Gaubert fumbled his sword and turned on his heel, running. His cousins, previously so ready to charge the two lithander with raised weapons, all scrambled after him, slipping in rain and mud.

Raffa fell to all fours, growling like an earthquake, ready to take chase.

"Raffa," Talos said.

Raffa paused long enough to look over his shoulder at his brother, and for a moment, Maëlle swore she saw his canine features soften. Brotherly love, as she'd known all along. "Keep her safe. I will see you at home." His eyes flicked to Maëlle for a fleeting second. "Both of you."

Talos nodded, once again arching a stone wing over Maëlle's head to protect her from rain. And then Raffa was charging after the fleeing Desroches men. In the wake of his leaving, the rain felt colder and heavier on Maëlle's skin, a shroud of storm settling over her. It was quieter without the larger lithander's presence, her hearing seemingly muffled despite the near constant thunder now.

Maëlle rubbed the afterimage of lightning from her eyes to look at the gentle, protective stone man standing next to her.

"Your wing," she said again, raising shaking fingers to smooth over the missing chip of stone. The edges were rough as snapped bone.

"I'm fine," Talos said quietly. "It doesn't hurt."

"Will it heal?"

He looked into the rain after his brother. "No. But I don't mind. Some scars are worth bearing."

Maëlle swallowed hard, past the lump in her throat. She knelt long enough to retrieve the stone feather from the puddle, letting it rest solidly in her palm. Something in her chest was begging to burst free for Talos to see, but she held herself together. She couldn't fall apart, not now, not in front of Talos. It would cut her more deeply than any axe if she did.

"Come with me," she said, taking Talos by the arm. "I know a place to wait out the storm."

Chapter Fourteen

The river caves were nowhere near as comfortable as Talos's home in the mountains. They were muddy and damp inside, smelling of mildew and algae, and the first one they tried had a nest of raccoons living at the back. But when they finally crouched in an empty cave, one that was not quite tall enough for Talos and his stone wings to stand upright in, there was a certain relief to being out of the rain and wind and lightning.

Everything felt quieter, stiller, gentler. The rain drummed distantly, but inside the stone space, the soft trickle of a tiny rivulet was infinitely more real.

Maëlle wrapped herself tightly in her soaked wool cloak, needing its warmth against the cave's chill. She nestled herself against Arwa's equally wet flank, searching for body heat among the fur and feathers. On the far side of the small cave, Talos sat on the sloped floor and propped his stone wings against the wall for balance. Between the night, the storm, and the cave, it was almost too dark to see him until he pulled a vial of foxfire lichen from the bag across his chest, casting the small space in a soft blue glow.

He was watching her, those jasper eyes almost purple with the reflection of blue light. His expression was so open and safe, so very much *him*, that she wanted to crawl into his lap and curl up there the way she had the night before, with her cheek pressed to his chest. But the distance between them felt like an insurmountable gulf, a space that stretched for miles. She thought if she let herself fall into that chasm, she would keep falling forever and never hit bottom.

"Would Gaubert really have killed you the day after your wedding?" he asked, soft voice unusually rough.

"Not the day after, no. But within the year, proba-bly." She pulled her cloak tighter around herself, trying to suppress the shiver. "He wants legitimate heirs, and I can't provide them."

Talos's mouth tightened, his shoulders going stiff. "Raffa was right about the Desroches," he said, shaking his head. "You won't go back?"

"Never." She said the word like slamming a door.

Talos looked down at his glowing vial, watching the light waver as he, too, seemed to waver. Unsure. He looked up at her through stone eyelashes, the shyness he had shed days ago back again. "Will you come home with me again?" he asked.

Maëlle split open. All her messy emotions—grief and longing and sadness and love too, of course love, so much love—spilled out of her like stones. She wondered that Talos couldn't see them, couldn't count the exact ways she felt by the colors and weights of those stones. How could she explain to Talos that she couldn't stand to live with him when he didn't return her feelings? How could she admit to loving him when he didn't love her back? Her heart gave a little lurch, and it caught as a sob in her throat.

"Talos," she said around the sob. She swallowed hard, tasting the bitter all the way down, and tried again. "Talos, emotions can be messy and raw and..." She trailed off, clenching his lost stone feather in her fist, not sure how to finish. Not sure how to tell him he had broken her heart.

"I've noticed," he agreed, pressing the palm of one stone hand against his chest.

She had to turn away from him, turn her face into the thick, wet fur of Arwa's side. When he looked at her that way, she felt herself coming apart. "I can't do it," she said, voice muffled against Arwa. "I can't. I meant what I said before, Talos. You deserve love, even if...even if it's not with me. But I can't...I can't..." She shook her head, tears threatening to overwhelm her. "Don't ask me to live both with you and without you, Talos. Don't ask me to watch you—to wait for you to—love someone else. It would break me." She thrust out her hand, offering the feather back to him on an open, shaking palm.

"Someone else? Why would...?" She heard him shift and turned to see the earnest determination painted on his face with such wide brushstrokes. "No, I'm not doing this right. I'm sorry, I've never..."

He rubbed the back of his neck, the sound of stone on stone shushing through the cave. His wings rustled anxiously behind him, the newly chipped spot pale as bone in the light of the foxfire lichen. Finally, he reached into his bag, pulling out items—jeweler's loupe, charcoal pencils, glass vials, measuring string—until he found the rectangle wrapped in waterproofed canvas at the bottom. Inside was one of his journals. Maëlle saw flashes of maps and landscapes as he flipped pages until he came to a loose piece of paper tucked between the pages of the book. He gingerly pulled it free, looking at it once, before offering it to Maëlle.

It was a half-finished painting of Arwa, the one he had been working on only yesterday. The gryphon was an indistinct outline, so far only the gray and brown suggestion of an animal. But in the center of the page, in perfect and minute detail, painted in syrupy golds and crisp blue, was Maëlle sitting against

Arwa and reading a book. Every strand of her hair and fold of her dress was perfect, the mouth painted a shade of rockrose pink and turned up in a small, private smile. She had never seen herself look so beautiful. With the rest of the painting only half finished, it made it look like Maëlle was the center of the universe, the only perfect thing in a faded world.

"But you were painting Arwa," she protested. She couldn't parse this picture, couldn't resolve what it meant. She was sure Talos was showing her some glimpse into himself, handing her his jeweler's loupe and opening a door into his deepest part for her to study, but she didn't know what she was seeing.

"I was painting Arwa," he agreed, "but I was memorizing you. Immortalizing you. It was always you."

Her head swam, her skin buzzing. "I don't...what?"

"Maëlle," he said, and his voice was very gentle and very serious and so very warm, and she could lose herself in those red jasper eyes. "I'm different since I met you. I'm metamorphic rock changing under high heat—stronger and softer both now. It's like...it's like you're a bee on alpine strawberries, and I am larger and lusher and sweeter for your presence. Or you're a glacial lake, reflecting all of me back to myself but with the crystalized light of sapphires sharpening it. Or you're a vibration in the air, a voice singing so purely that I vibrate with you, a tuning fork in the same key. You build fires in me, Maëlle. You construct magma, forge volcanoes, fill me with the light and heat of suns, of stars, of entire galaxies."

Talos was speaking poetry, a string of gem-cut metaphors, each more beautiful than the last. She could curl up in his words and die in dazzled splendor. But words had meaning, and she didn't understand his. He was looking at her with the earnestness of someone speaking a different language but willing her to understand nonetheless, like he could cut the heart out of his words and bind it in a book for her to read. It left her breathless and shaky and...

"No," she managed, her voice a fragile thing. She saw again, in her memory, the moments after she had bared her deepest insecurity and Talos moved back out of her reach. The sharp stone edges of his broken feather pressed against her clenched hand, threatening to slice her palm open. "You pulled back from me. You learned that I'm broken, and you ran from me." The memory was like being stabbed by betrayal all over again, and her voice broke on the last words.

The look of shock split Talos's expression. "No!" he said, sitting forward with the fervor of his insistence. "That's not why I ran! I was...in turmoil. You said so many things, explained things that made brilliant sense but also created chaos in me. Contradictions and expansions of scope, new perspectives. I couldn't think straight, couldn't organize my head. I was one soft touch away from falling to pieces."

He paused, pressing his hands to his head in the same way he had yesterday in the strawberry garden when Maëlle was explaining about love, like he was afraid he might fly apart if he didn't physically hold himself together. "I'm so sorry. I should have known how it would look for me to leave then, but I'm...I'm so bad at this, Maëlle. I'm sorry, and I'm sorry, and I'm sorry. I don't know the words strong enough to apologize properly. You're not broken, and I'm terrible for making you feel like you are. I wasn't running from you. I was running from me, from the buzzing in my brain, but that's no excuse for making you feel that way. I would never run from you, Maëlle."

She was shaking her head, trying to fit his words with what she remembered, looking at the same painful scene over and over again, through all the distorting facets of a jewel with edges cut so sharply they could make you bleed. "You sent Raffa to turn me away, to tell me to..." She trailed off, remembering now what Talos had said earlier, just before Gaubert had interrupted them.

"I wasn't there!" Talos insisted. "I never asked Raffa to send you away."

"But he said..." What had Raffa said? Nothing directly. He had implied a lot through word and body language. He had said things that she knew matched his own opinions. But he had never directly confirmed Talos was there. And if he had been gone then, if Talos hadn't known Gaubert was coming, how could Talos have any blame for Raffa's actions?

"Raffa was carved to fight humans in the wars," Talos said quietly. "He's gruff and grumpy, but he's a better person than he pretends to be. Raffa was the one to show me where Desroches Manor is."

Raffa's last reluctant words before he chased Gaubert echoed brittle in her head: "Both of you."

She wrapped her arms around her middle, her stomach alternately feeling as empty as a void and expanding with the heat of a furnace. What did this all mean? Talos had lots of pretty words, metaphors as detailed as his sketches and notebooks, but he hadn't really said anything certain. She could be important to him without emotion involved—a specimen for study or a pet like Raffa had said. But... Something flickered in her chest. She remembered the feeling when he had kissed her by the lake, the glacier dropping pieces of ice into the water, the careful picnic spread around them, the sun dazzling them both. She remembered when he held her by the fire. She had felt safe, yes, and comfortable—but she also had been convinced there was something else germinating in the spaces between them.

"Talos," she said, squeezing herself tighter. "I don't..." She trailed off, afraid to ask, afraid to force his hand in case the fragile thing in the air between them was shattered.

"I spent a lot of time thinking about what you said," Talos said. "Among the strawberries, when you were trying so hard to explain love to me. That love is passion, a desire to protect and make someone happy and spend time with them. That someone you love feels like they belong or fit with you, that they feel *right* next to you. Maëlle, I've never recognized passion in myself before meeting you. I've never wanted companionship more than the lonely mountains. You do feel right next to me. You feel so right that not having you there feels wrong."

Something in Maëlle's chest—her heart? hope? love?—was expanding and expanding. It pressed out against her rib cage in something that was part pain and part exquisite pleasure, and she couldn't breathe with it. She wanted the moment of lovely suffering to last for eternity, and she wanted to burst the bubble immediately, and most of all, what she really wanted was...

"What are you saying, Talos?" she asked, words a breathless quavering mix of hope and fear.

"I'm saying— I'm saying— I'm saying..."

Talos came forward towards her, kneeling in the mud of the cave. His jasper eyes were red and steady and somehow softer than any stone had a right to be. His face was so open she could see meadows in it, verdant expanses of nodding wildflowers and grass. He kept his hands clutched together, to his chest, just below his throat, held so gently he could have a trapped butterfly between them. He made a noise, something that sounded like the shifting of distant ice, and his wings spread up and behind him until they brushed the ceiling, the white stone veins in his new injury sparkling like a million tiny stars. The blue light of the foxfire lichen from behind limned all his stone in a soft halo. He was a faerie, or an angel, or a god. He was the most beautiful thing she had ever seen, a statue carved not of stone but of pure grace and sweetness and hope.

"I'm saying that I love you, Maëlle. I love you."

The great pushing expansion in her chest escaped as a sob, and she flung herself at him, wrapping her arms around his neck like she couldn't be bruised. And she pressed her lips to his, hard and hot, felt him open under her, felt him heat up and soften for her, as pliant as clay under her fingertips and lips. He wrapped one arm around her waist, and it was a lifeline holding her to him. His other hand was in her hair, sending shivers through her scalp as strands of hair ran over the rough granite surfaces. He kissed her back, and for a moment the whole universe lived between their lips, and they were there to discover it, to unfold it, to let it bloom.

She paused long enough to gasp for breath against his mouth, just barely long enough to say, "I love you too, Talos. I love you so much."

They kissed like desperation and tenderness and fragile newness. They kissed like the sun on mountaintops and warm summer strawberries and hauntingly lovely music by a fireplace. They kissed like avalanches, like volcanoes, like combustion. They kissed like they could never kiss enough, like there wasn't enough time in the world, like it was the only thing that mattered. They kissed until the thunder and lightning faded off into the distance, barely a memory of rumbles, until the rain stopped drumming, until the only sound of water was the slow drips of a clean world. They kissed until the sky lightened to pale orange-pink outside the cave, and the morning birds sang them into a new day.

Eventually, Arwa woke and went outside to hunt, and Maëlle curled up against Talos, soaking in the blissful heat that radiated from him. This was new. He had always been warmer than she expected, but not as much as this. The more they kissed, the warmer he got until it seemed they both should be incinerated, and still, it felt good.

Talos used his gentlest touch to move a strand of hair from her face, watching her carefully. "Will you come home with me again?" he asked, as he had before, and this time, instead of breaking Maëlle open, it bound her together.

"It would be inconvenient for you," she pointed out, but she said it tenderly, tracing the feather she still held with one finger. Hesitantly, she held it out for him again, an offering. "I need so many more things than you do—clothes and food and water and heat. A bed would be nice."

He looked at the stone feather in her flesh palm, making no move to take it. "I can give you all of that. I would move the mountains to make you comfortable, and it would be no burden. But there would be things I can't give you, too. Marriage, for one—lithander don't marry. Sex. I can't even grow old with you since lithander don't age."

"But you can give me your love."

"You already have it."

"And I can give you love, too."

"Is that enough?" he asked, so timid and gentle and earnest, and oh sweet lord she loved this man.

"Enough?" she asked, laughing with the brightness of summer sunshine. "It's more than enough. It's everything."

He cupped her cheek with one of his hands, still so gentle, like he might bruise her with no more than a thought. "Is that a yes?" he asked.

"Yes, Talos. That's a yes."

Gently, he closed her hand around his lost stone feather until she clutched it to her chest. And she kissed him again as the new day bloomed soft and sweet and shivering in anticipation of what came next.

Epilogue

Talos watched the bees. The ones leaving the hive were agile and frisky, and those returning were clumsy with the burden of full pollen baskets on their legs. They were always so busy, these bees, up with the sun and buzzing away in their hive at night. He was glad he had decided to add the beehive this year. It was the first time he had watched the insects so carefully, and he appreciated the chance to study the industrious creatures up close, from egg to adult. He had seen queens and drones and workers, tiny larvae and the eggs they hatched from. He had watched the bees make honey and feed pollen to the babies, had seen them work together to chase away hornets or repair damage after a hailstorm. He had filled an entire journal with sketches and observations and notes on the bees this summer. Much longer, and he'd have to start a second one.

Not to mention having the beehive increased the yield of the garden. There were strawberries again, but the garden had also grown, a rambling patch of lettuce and peas, potatoes and beans, trailing squash and bunched herbs, transplanted patches of wild burdock and stonecrop onions and bunchberries. Food for Maëlle; food for his love.

Overhead, Arwa made a screech as she circled—no saddle or rider today. The gryphon had taken to exploring the mountains and hunting for small prey, though she always came when Maëlle called. He smiled, never tired of seeing the gryphon's graceful flight.

He closed his journal and tucked it into his bag, leaving the bees to their work as the sun finished rising over the mountain peaks. He picked a handful of strawberries and climbed down the steps cut into the stone. He had spent months carving those steps. They were worth every moment of his time.

He heard Maëlle before he saw her, and as always, her sad-sweet singing brought an ache to his chest and a smile to his face. She was in the mossy courtyard of their home, singing a song about faeries while she shaped a bit of clay into a bowl.

This was her new hobby—pottery. Utilitarian, sure, in that she needed vessels to eat and drink and cook, but she shaped them with hard edges and pressed them with soft flowers and leaves before firing them, and they were a beautiful juxtaposition when done. She sold extras in the nearest town, along with Talos's paintings and rudimentary stone carvings, when they needed to barter for the things they couldn't find or make for themselves. Paints and inks, metal cooking pots, new blank journals to fill, books to read. A bed with a soft mattress.

For a moment, Talos stopped on the stairs and watched Maëlle work. He still sometimes had trouble believing this was his life. He had love and companionship and happiness, and each day was a new gift crystalizing out of the mountain air, sparkling with the sapphire color of Maëlle's eyes. He still ached to have her by him in all the best ways possible. No one had told him that love kept growing larger and larger.

Maëlle's song came to a heartrending crescendo, the bittersweet ending reverberating in the air like gold. He wanted to gather it in his palms, spin it to spider silk, and save it for later. But she would sing again. She always sang again. So he let the fading notes wash over him instead.

"Do all of the faerie songs have sad endings?" he asked, finally walking down the rest of the steps. She turned and smiled at him, blue eyes sparkling and hair a halo of gold. She had a smear of clay on one cheek, and he used a gentle thumb to wipe it away.

"I don't think they're sad."

He offered her a small heart-shaped strawberry, and since her hands were slick with clay to the wrists, he let her take it from his palm with her teeth. "Faerie princes who lose their immortality. Maidens turned to trees for decades while their love was lost in the faerie lands. Faerie lovers turned to salt while kissing. You don't think those are sad?"

"Bittersweet, maybe. But in all of them, love wins, no matter the obstacles." She gave him such a tender look then, and he thought he would melt at her feet. "That's why I like them so much."

If Talos had needed to breathe, that would have knocked the air from him. All this time, and she could still surprise him—could still make him think about something in a new way, or appreciate something he had ignored before, could give him a fresh insight. She could still turn him inside out without warning.

Maybe now was the time, he thought.

"I want to show you something," he said and suddenly felt as shy as he had been when they first met, when he had thought she was so fragile and worried about the world hurting her. The more he lived with Maëlle, the more he realized how resilient she was. She could bruise, but she healed, too. "Wait here a moment."

He gave her a quick kiss, leaving her to clean the clay from her hands as he went into their home—the new home, the one they had made for themselves. They left the previous small cave to Raffa and his carving, though Talos's brother was only on the next mountain peak, close enough they could yell conversations back and forth across the chasm if needed. He might put a bridge in someday, connecting their mountain home to the peak where Raffa lived. It would make trips to visit a matter of moments. Maybe when Raffa was done carving his son. He had been taking his time with the project, months gone and barely any change in the block of granite. Talos didn't blame him. Creating a new life was not a small task, and it deserved care and dedication.

They had lined one stone wall of their home with bookshelves, displaying a mix of his journals and the books Maëlle liked to read. He ran a stone finger down the spines until he found the sketchbook he was looking for, pulling it free. He paused for a moment, fingertips running over the leather cover. Hesitated. But what was there to hesitate about? Why was he so nervous? Maëlle already loved him, after all.

He brought the book outside, where Maëlle was drying her cleaned hands. The early sun was copper on her skin. She smiled at him again, and he knew he would never get enough of those rockrose-colored lips showing pleasure for him. Sometimes he thought the love inside him might grow big enough to burst, and it would be a blissful way to die.

"Is this it?" she asked, holding out a hand for the sketchbook. "What you wanted to show me?"

Again, Talos hesitated, feeling small and shy and unsure. "It's...not much, but..." He stared at the blank cover again, then held it out.

He couldn't watch her flip through the pages, couldn't see her reaction—but he also couldn't look away. With each page, her eyes grew larger and fuller, whole worlds unraveling in their depths. She pressed a hand to her chest, just where she wore his broken stone feather on a necklace over her heart, like she could keep her heartbeat from escaping. She sat on one of their stone benches as if she could no longer bear to fight gravity, and her bare toes dug into the moss for its softness.

"Talos," she said, looking up at him with a wonder alight on her face as ethereal as fireflies. "What is this?"

He sat next to her, running a hand over the page she had left open so that the book was flat. On it, a sketch: a female form, human face and body, but long tresses of owl feathers for hair and a spreading set of owl wings behind. The bodice was traced with the shapes of ferns and flowers, the eyes set as polished sapphires. The figure looked like Maëlle but also didn't look quite human. It was a statue carved of stone, but also looked softer than stone should be.

Talos bit a lip, tracing the sketch's curved wing with one fingertip. "You've seen Raffa at work. You know how lithander are created. I'm not ready to carve a child yet, but someday..." He flipped to another rendition of the figure, then another, each subtly different but each still showing pieces of Maëlle, pieces of Talos, pieces of both twined into one person. "I was hoping you would help with it when I'm ready."

He wasn't sure if this was the right thing to do, the right thing to ask. He still didn't quite understand human reproduction or the way Maëlle felt about children. Most of the time, he treaded lightly around the topics, afraid to cause more harm, even unintentionally, the way he had that day she explained love to him. The worst thing he could do was hurt her. It had made him scared to share this idea, this hope with her. Even as he said it, he wasn't sure what her response would be.

But he watched the way Maëlle took in a breath like she had never breathed before, watched her expression open like a new spring flower, watched her eyes shimmer with unshed tears until the blue was magnified to a heartrending degree. He saw the hope and the wonder unfurl in her expression, the beautiful way she took his idea into her heart and wrapped it in soft layers of herself. And he knew the idea had taken root and that she would care for it as tenderly as a newly germinated seedling.

"I would love that," she said, leaning her head against his shoulder.

How did he deserve this woman, he wondered. How did he deserve this love? It was bigger than the world, brighter than the sun, and purer than glacial meltwater, and he would never let it go. Next to him, Maëlle ran soft fingers over the charcoal lines of his drawing, a bittersweet and lovely smile on her lips. And there was nowhere Talos would rather be, nowhere but here, with Maëlle next to him, dreaming of a shared future and building mountains of love between them.

Acknowledgements

Thanks for reading my book, and I hope you enjoyed it! This book owes gratitude to a multitude of sources, and wouldn't be what it is now without the influences, support, and assistance of so many wonderful people. I want to take a moment to thank a few in particular, though there are dozens more that have helped in their own way.

First, Worldsmyths (and penguinball in particular) were the initial inspiration for writing a romance story, which I had never done before. Thanks for pushing me to try a new genre and discover I love writing about love. And thanks to the group as a whole (and members including Ally, Sheepy, and Shannon) for helping me navigate the self-publishing process. It's been a lot to figure out, but much easier with friends!

My earliest readers, including Odessa/Sheepy, Isa, Amanda, and several members of the Fantasy and Sci-Fi Writers Alliance (Matt, Cecilia, Anthony, and Ashley), were so helpful for a tone check and early encouragement.

J. S. Elliot, Kat, and C. P. Miller – my amazing critique group – provided excellent feedback, conversation, and suggestions for revisions, and this book wouldn't be as good as it is without their help. I'm so lucky to have such a constructive, knowledgeable, and entertaining critique group!

Thanks to my editor, Charlie Knight, for their careful attention to detail and excellent big-picture comments. One of my favorite scenes in the book is as strong as it is thanks to their feedback (they know which one!).

Special thanks to my cover designer, Asterielly, who donated a cover package to an auction to raise funds in Western North Carolina after Hurricane Helene.

Last but obviously not least, thanks to my family for being continually supportive and understanding as I not only wrote this book but figured out how to self-publish it. They've been patient and encouraging through the whole process. In particular, E. and O., I love you both from the bedrock to the moon.

About the Author

Nicole Leland is a fantasy romance author who shares a brain (quite literally) with fantasy and science fiction author Nicole L. Soper Gorden. She enjoys writing about nature almost as much as she enjoys writing about love. When she's not writing, you can find Nicole daydreaming more than she should, reading voraciously, baking sweet treats for loved ones, or waxing poetic about plant reproduction. She lives a romantic life of her own in the mountains with her husband and child.

How to Follow Nicole

Keep up with Nicole's writing journey on the following platforms:

- www.NicoleLSoperGorden.com

- Sign up for her newsletter

- Follow on social media:

  - **Instagram** (@NicoleLSoperGorden)

  - **Bluesky** (@NicoleLSoperGorden)

  - **Facebook** (@NicoleLSoperGorden)

Also by Nicole Leland

If you enjoyed this book and are looking for another sweet romance with a darker tone, make sure to check out Hearts of Bark and Scale by Nicole Leland, coming out October 27, 2025.

Other Stories

In the mood for general fantasy and science fiction stories by the same author? Check out some of the published short stories by **Nicole L. Soper Gorden** (my general non-romance pen name)!

- **"Tea for Truth, Mango for Memory"** available in Beneath Ceaseless Skies

- **"The Hundred Names of Atiya Djinn"** available in Written in the Wind

- **"Into the Breaking Season"** available in Seasons Unceasing

- **The Silver King and the Jade Egg"** available in Gilded Glass

- **"When the Raven Ate the Moons"** available in

Darkness and Moonlight

- **"Sweetening the Deal"** available in Myths, Legends, and Dreams

- **"Sing a Song of Sixpence"** available in Dreams and Deceit